MIGHT AS WELL BE DEAD

It was just an innocent search for a missing person. Well, we found him all right—in the death cell of a city prison—accused of murder. Surprise is not an expression I expect from Nero Wolfe, but this time you could have knocked him over with a baby orchid.

BEFORE WE KNEW IT WE WERE MIXED UP IN A CLEVER EMBEZZLEMENT, A MURDER, A BIG FAT NATIONAL SCANDAL, AND MORE MURDER, MUCH MORE MURDER!

A NERO WOLFE NOVEL

MIGHT AS WELL BE DEAD

BY REX STOUT

BANTAM BOOKS · TORONTO · LONDON · NEW YORK

MIGHT AS WELL BE DEAD

A Bantam Book / published by arrangement with
The Viking Press Inc.

PRINTING HISTORY

Viking Press edition published October 1956
Dollar Mystery Guild edition published February 1957

Bantam edition / July 1958

2nd printing	January 1967	4th printing	January 1977
3rd printing	March 1974	5th printing	October 1980

Bantam Books are published by Bantam Books, Inc. Its trade-
mark, consisting of the words "Bantam Books" and the por-
trayal of a bantam, is Registered in U.S. Patent and Trademark
Office and in other countries. Marca Registrada. Bantam
Books, Inc., 666 Fifth Avenue, New York, New York 10103.

PRINTED IN THE UNITED STATES OF AMERICA

14 13 12 11 10 9 8 7 6 5

MIGHT AS WELL BE DEAD

Most of the people who come to see Nero Wolfe by appointment, especially from as far away as Nebraska, show some sign of being in trouble, but that one didn't. With his clear unwrinkled skin and alert brown eyes and thin straight mouth, he didn't even look his age. I knew his age, sixty-one. When a telegram had come from James R. Herold, Omaha, Nebraska, asking for an appointment Monday afternoon, of course I had checked on him. He was sole owner of the Herold Hardware Company, wholesale, a highly respected citizen, and rated at over half a million—a perfect prospect for a worthy fee if he had real trouble. Seeing him had been a letdown. From his looks, he might merely be after a testimonial for a gadget to trim orchid plants. He had settled back comfortably in the red leather chair.

"I guess," he said, "I'd better tell you why I picked you."

"As you please," Wolfe muttered from behind his desk. For half an hour after lunch he never gets above a mutter unless he has to.

Herold crossed his legs. "It's about my son. I want to find my son. About a month ago I put ads in the New York papers, and I contacted the New York police, and— What's the matter?"

"Nothing. Go on."

It was not nothing. Wolfe had made a face. I, at my desk, could have told Herold that unless his problem smelled like real money he might as well quit right there. One man who had made "contact" a verb in that office had paid an extra thousand bucks for the privilege, though he hadn't known it.

Herold looked doubtful; then his face cleared. "Oh. You don't like poking in a police matter, but that's all right. I've been keeping after the Missing Persons Bureau, a Lieutenant Murphy, and I've run some more newspaper ads in the Personals, but they've got no results at all, and my wife was getting impatient about it, so I phoned Lieutenant Murphy from Omaha and told him I wanted to hire a private detective agency and asked him to recommend one. He said he couldn't do that, but I can be pretty determined when I want to, and he gave me your name. He said that on a job like finding a missing person you yourself wouldn't be much because you were too fat and lazy, but that you had two men, one named Archie Goodwin and one named Saul Panzer, who were tops for that kind of work. So I wired you for an appointment."

Wolfe made the noise he uses for a chuckle, and moved a finger to indicate me. "This is Mr. Goodwin. Tell him about it."

"He's in your employ, isn't he?"

"Yes. My confidential assistant."

"Then I'll tell you. I like to deal with principals. My son Paul is my only son—I have two daughters. When he graduated from college, the University of Nebraska, I took him into my business, wholesale hardware. That was in nineteen forty-five, eleven years ago. He had been a little wild in college, but I thought he would settle into the harness, but he didn't. He stole twenty-six thousand dollars of the firm's money, and I kicked him out." His straight thin mouth tightened a little. "Out of the business and out of the house. He left Omaha and I never saw him again. I didn't want to see him, but now I do and my wife does. One month ago, on March eighth, I learned that he didn't take that money. I learned who did, and it has been proven beyond all doubt. That's being attended to, the thief is being taken care of, and now I want to find my son." He got a large envelope from his pocket, took things from it, and left his chair. "That's a picture of him, taken in June nineteen forty-five, the latest one I have." He handed me one too. "Here are six copies of it, and of course I can get more." He returned to the chair and sat. "He got a raw deal and I want to make it square with him.

I have nothing to apologize for, because at the time there was good evidence that he had taken the money, but now I know he didn't and I've got to find him. My wife is very impatient about it."

The picture was of a round-cheeked kid in a mortar-board and gown, with a dimple in his chin. No visible resemblance to his father. As for the father, he certainly wasn't being maudlin. You could say he was bearing up well in the circumstances, or you could say he was plain cold fish. I preferred the latter.

Wolfe dropped the picture on the desk top. "Evidently," he muttered, "you think he's in New York. Why?"

"Because every year my wife and daughters have been getting cards from him on their birthdays—you know, those birthday cards. I suspected all along that my wife was corresponding with him, but she says not. She admits she would have, but he never gave her an address. He never wrote her except the cards, and they were all postmarked New York."

"When did the last one come?"

"November nineteenth, less than five months ago. My daughter Marjorie's birthday. Postmarked New York like the others."

"Anything else? Has anyone ever seen him here?"

"Not that I know of."

"Have the police made any progress?"

"No. None whatever. I'm not complaining; I guess they've tried; but of course in a great city like this they've got their hands full of problems and I'm only one. I'm pretty sure he came straight to New York from Omaha, by train, back eleven years ago, but I haven't been able to verify it. The police had several men on it for a week, or they said they had, but now I think they've only got one, and I agree with my wife that I've got to do something. I've been neglecting my business."

"That will never do," Wolfe said dryly. Apparently he favored the cold-fish slant too. "And no results from the newspaper advertisements?"

"No. I got letters from five detective agencies offering to help me—of course the replies were to a box number—and quite a few, at least two dozen, from crackpots and impostors. The police investigated all of them, and they were all duds."

"How were the advertisements worded?"

"I wrote them myself. They were all alike." Herold got a big leather wallet from his breast pocket, fished in it, and extracted a clipping. He twisted in his chair to get better light from a window, and read:

Paul Herold, who left Omaha, Nebraska, in 1945, will learn something to his advantage by communicating with his father immediately. It has been learned that a mistake was made. Also anyone who sees this ad and knows anything of the said Paul Herold's whereabouts, either now or at any time during the past ten years, is requested to communicate and a proper reward will be given.

X904 Times.

"I ran that in five New York papers." He returned the clipping to the wallet and the wallet to the pocket. "Thirty times altogether. Money wasted. I don't mind spending money, but I hate to waste it."

Wolfe grunted. "You might waste it on me—or on Mr. Goodwin and Mr. Panzer. Your son may have changed his name on arrival in New York—indeed, that seems likely, since neither the police nor the advertisements have found any trace of him. Do you know if he took luggage with him when he left Omaha?"

"Yes, he took all his clothes and some personal things. He had a trunk and a suitcase and a bag."

"Were his initials on any of it?"

"His initials?" Herold frowned. "Why—Oh, yes. They were on the trunk and the suitcase, presents from his mother. My wife. Why?"

"Just PH, or a middle initial?"

"He had no middle name. Just PH. Why?"

"Because if he changed his name he probably found it convenient to keep the PH. Initials on luggage have dictated ten thousand aliases. Even so, Mr. Herold, assuming the PH, it is a knotty and toilsome job, for we must also assume that your son prefers not to be found, since the advertisements failed to flush him. I suggest that you let him be."

"You mean quit looking for him?"

"Yes."

"I can't. My wife, and my daughters—Anyway, I won't. Right is right. I've got to find him."

"And you want to hire me?"

"Yes. You and Goodwin and Panzer."

"Then I must inform you that it may take months, the expenses will be considerable, the amount of my bill will not be contingent on success, and I charge big fees."

"I know you do. Lieutenant Murphy told me." Herold looked more like a man in trouble than when he came in. "But I can call you off at any time."

"Certainly."

"All right." He took a breath. "You want a retainer."

"As an advance for expenses. More important, I want all the information you can give me." Wolfe's head turned. "Archie, your notebook."

I already had it out.

An hour later, after the client had left and Wolfe had gone up to the plant rooms for his afternoon session with Theodore and the orchids, I put the check for three thousand dollars in the safe and then got at the typewriter to transcribe my notes. When I was done I had five pages of assorted facts, one or two of which might possibly be useful. Paul Herold had a three-inch scar on his left leg, on the inside of the knee, from a boyhood accident. That might help if we found him with his pants down. It had made him 4F and kept him out of war. His mother had called him Poosie. He had liked girls, and had for a time concentrated on one at college named Arline Macy, but had not been hooked, and so far as was known had communicated with none after heading east. He had majored in Social Science, but on that his father had been a little vague. He had taken violin lessons for two years and then sold the violin for twenty bucks, and got hell for it. He had tried for football in spite of his bum knee, but didn't make the team, and in baseball had played left field for two innings against Kansas in 1944. No other sports to speak of. Smoke and drink, not to excess. Gambling, not to the client's knowledge. He had always pushed some on his allowance, but there had been nothing involving dishonesty or other moral turpitude before the blow-up.

And so on and so forth. It didn't look very promising. Evidence of some sort of dedication, such as a love for animals that hop or a determination to be President of the United States, might have helped a little, but it wasn't there. If his father had really known him, which I doubted, he had been just an ordinary kid who had had a rotten piece of luck, and now it was anybody's guess what he had turned into. I decided that I didn't appreciate the plug Lieutenant Murphy of the Missing Persons Bureau had given me, along with Saul Panzer. Any member of the NYPD, from Commissioner Skinner on down, would have given a day's pay, after taxes, to see Nero Wolfe stub his toe, and it seemed likely that Murphy, after spending a month on it, had figured that this was a fine prospect. I went to the kitchen and told Fritz we had taken on a job that would last two years and would be a washout.

Fritz smiled and shook his head. "No washouts in this house," he said positively. "Not with Mr. Wolfe and you both here." He got a plastic container from the refrigerator, took it to the table, and removed the lid.

"Hey," I protested, "we had shad roe for lunch! Again for dinner?"

"My dear Archie." He was superior, to me, only about food. "They were merely sauté, with a simple little sauce, only chives and chervil. These will be en casserole, with anchovy butter made by me. The sheets of larding will be rubbed with five herbs. With the cream to cover will be an onion and three other herbs, to be removed before serving. The roe season is short, and Mr. Wolfe could enjoy it three times a day. You can go to Al's place on Tenth Avenue and enjoy a ham on rye with coleslaw." He shuddered.

It developed into an argument, but I avoided getting out on a limb, not wanting to have to drop off into Al's place. We were still at it when, at six o'clock, I heard the elevator bringing Wolfe down from the plant rooms, and after winding it up with no hard feelings I left Fritz to his sheets of larding and went back to the office.

Wolfe was standing over by the bookshelves, looking at the globe, which was even bigger around than he was, checking to make sure that Omaha, Nebraska, was where it always had been. That done, he crossed over to his desk, and around it, and lowered his colossal corpus into his custom-made chair.

He cocked his head to survey the Feraghan, which covered all the central expanse, 14 x 26. "It's April," he said, "and that rug's dirty. I must remind Fritz to send it to be cleaned and put the others down."

"Yeah," I agreed, looking down at him. "But for a topic for discussion that won't last long. If you want to avoid discussing Paul Herold start something with some body to it, like the Middle East."

He grunted. "I don't have to avoid it. According to Lieutenant Murphy, that's for you and Saul. Have you reached Saul?"

"Yes. We're going to disguise ourselves as recruiting officers for the Salvation Army. He starts at the Battery and works north, and I start at Van Cortlandt Park and work south. We'll meet at Grant's Tomb on Christmas Eve and compare notes, and then start in on Brooklyn. Have you anything better to suggest?"

"I'm afraid not." He sighed, deep. "It may be hopeless. Has that Lieutenant Murphy any special reason to bear me a grudge?"

"It doesn't have to be special. He's a cop, that's enough."

"I suppose so." He shut his eyes, and in a moment opened them again. "I should have declined the job. Almost certainly he has never been known in New York as Paul Herold. That picture is eleven years old. What does he look like now? It's highly probable that he doesn't want to be found and, if so, he has been put on the alert by the advertisements. The police are well qualified for the task of locating a missing person, and if after a full month they—Get Lieutenant Murphy on the phone."

I went to my desk and dialed CA 6-2000, finally persuaded a sergeant that only Murphy would do, and, when I had him, signaled to Wolfe. I stayed on.

"Lieutenant Murphy? This is Nero Wolfe. A man named James R. Herold, of Omaha, Nebraska, called on me this afternoon to engage me to find his son Paul. He said you had given him my name. He also said your bureau has been conducting a search for his son for about a month. Is that correct?"

"That's correct. Did you take the job?"

"Yes."

"Fine. Good luck, Mr. Wolfe."

"Thank you. May I ask, did you make any progress?"

"None whatever. All we got was dead ends."

"Did your search go beyond your set routine?"

"That depends on what you call routine. It was a clear-cut case and the boy had had a rough deal, and you could say we made a special effort. I've still got a good man on it. If you want to send Goodwin down with a letter from Herold we'll be glad to show him the reports."

"Thank you. You have no suggestions?"

"I'm afraid not. Good luck."

Wolfe didn't thank him again. We hung up.

"Swell," I said. "He thinks he's handed you a gazookis. The hell of it is, he's probably right. So where do we start?"

"Not at the Battery," Wolfe growled.

"Okay, but where? It may even be worse than we think. What if Paul framed himself for the theft of the twenty-six grand so as to have an excuse to get away from father? Having met father, I would buy that. And seeing the ad asking him to communicate with father—not mentioning mother or sisters, just father—and saying a mistake was made, what does he do? He either beats it to Peru or the the Middle East—there's the Middle East again—or he goes and buys himself a set of whiskers. That's an idea; we can check on all sales of whiskers in the last month, and if we find—"

"Shut up. It is an idea."

I stared. "My God, it's not that desperate. I was merely trying to stir your blood up and get your brain started, as usual, and if you—"

"I said shut up. Is it too late to get an advertisement into tomorrow's papers?"

"The Gazette, no. The Times, maybe."

"Your notebook."

Even if he had suddenly gone batty, I was on his payroll. I went to my desk, got the notebook, turned to a fresh page, and took my pen.

"Not in the classified columns," he said. "A display two columns wide and three inches high. Headed 'To P.H.' in large boldface, with periods after the P and H. Then this text, in smaller type: 'Your innocence is known and the injustice done you is regretted.'" He paused. "Change the 'regretted' to 'deplored.' Resume: 'Do not let bitterness prevent righting of a wrong.'" Pause again. "'No unwelcome contact will be urged upon you, but your help is needed to expose the true culprit. I engage to honor your reluctance to resume any tie you have renounced.'"

He pursed his lips a moment, then nodded. "That will do. Followed by my name and address and phone number."

"Why not mention mother?" I asked.

"We don't know how he feels toward his mother."

"He sent her birthday cards."

"By what impulsion? Do you know?"

"No."

"Then it would be risky. We can safely assume only two emotions for him: resentment of the wrong done him, and a desire to avenge it. If he lacks those he is less or more than human, and we'll never find him. I am aware, of course, that this is a random shot at an invisible target and a hit would be a prodigy. Have you other suggestions?"

I said no and swiveled the typewriter to me.

2

At any given moment there are probably 38,437 people in the metropolitan area who have been unjustly accused of something, or think they have, and 66 of them have the initials P.H. One-half of the 66, or 33, saw that ad, and one-third of the 33, or 11, answered it—three of them by writing letters, six by phoning, and two by calling in person at the old brownstone house on West 35th Street, Manhattan, which Wolfe owns, inhabits, and dominates except when I decide that he has gone too far.

The first reaction was not from a P.H. but an L.C.— Lon Cohen of the *Gazette*. He phoned Tuesday morning and asked what the line was on the Hays case. I said we had no line on any Hays case, and he said nuts.

He went on. "Wolfe runs an ad telling P.H. he knows he's innocent, but you have no line? Come on, come on. After all the favors I've done you? All I ask is—"

I cut him off. "Wrong number. But I should have known, and so should Mr. Wolfe. We do read the papers, so we know a guy named Peter Hays is on trial for murder. Not our P.H. But it could be a damn nuisance. I hope to God he doesn't see the ad."

"Okay. You're sitting on it, and when Wolfe's sitting on something it's being sat on good. But when you're ready to loosen up, think of me. My name is Damon, Pythias."

Since there was no use trying to convince him, I skipped it. I didn't buzz Wolfe, who was up in the plant rooms for his morning exercise, to ride him for not remembering there was a P.H. being tried for murder, because I should have remembered it myself.

The other P.H.'s kept me busy, off and on, most of the day. One named Phillip Horgan was no problem, because he came in person and one look was enough. He was somewhat older than our client. The other one who came in person, while we were at lunch, was tougher. His name was Perry Hettinger, and he refused to believe the ad wasn't aimed at him. By the time I got rid of him and returned to the dining room Wolfe had cleaned up the kidney pie and I got no second helping.

The phone calls were more complicated, since I couldn't see the callers. I eliminated three of them through appropriate and prolonged conversation, but the other three had to have a look, so I made appointments to see them; and since I had to stick around I phoned Saul Panzer, who came and got one of the pictures father had left and went to keep the appointments. It was an insult to Saul to give him such a kindergarten assignment, considering that he is the best operative alive and rates sixty bucks a day, but the client had asked for him and it was the client's dough.

The complication of a P.H.'s being on trial for murder was as big a nuisance as I expected, and then some. All the papers phoned, including the *Times*, and two of them sent journalists to the door, where I chatted with them on the threshold. Around noon there was a phone call from Sergeant Purley Stebbins of Homicide. He wanted to speak to Wolfe, and I said Mr. Wolfe was engaged, which he was. He was working on a crossword puzzle by Ximenes in the London *Observer*. I asked Purley if I could help him.

"You never have yet," he rumbled. "But neither has Wolfe. But when he runs a display ad telling a man on trial for murder that he knows he's innocent and he wants to expose the true culprit, we want to know what he's trying to pull and we're going to. If he won't tell me on the phone I'll be there in ten minutes."

"I'll be glad to save you the trip," I assured him. "Tell you what. You wouldn't believe me anyway, so call Lieutenant Murphy at the Missing Persons Bureau. He'll tell you all about it."

"What kind of a gag is this?"

"No gag. I wouldn't dare to trifle with an officer of the law. Call Murphy. If he doesn't satisfy you come and have lunch with us. Peruvian melon, kidney pie, endive with Martinique dressing—"

It clicked and he was gone. I turned and told Wolfe it would be nice if we could always get Stebbins off our neck as easy as that. He frowned a while at the London *Observer* and then raised his head.

"Archie."

"Yes, sir."

"That trial, that Peter Hays, started about two weeks ago."

"Right."

"The *Times* had his picture. Get it."

I grinned at him. "Wouldn't that be something? It popped into my head too, the possibility, when Lon phoned, but I remembered the pictures of him—the

Gazette and *Daily News*, all of them, and I crossed it off. But it won't hurt to look."

One of my sixteen thousand duties is keeping a five-week file of the *Times* in a cupboard below the bookshelves. I went and slid the door open and squatted, and before long I had it, on the seventeenth page of the issue of March 27. I gave it a look and went and handed it to Wolfe, and from a drawer of my desk got the picture of Paul Herold in mortarboard and gown, and handed him that too. He held them side by side and scowled at them, and I circled around to his elbow to help. The newspaper shot wasn't any too good, but even so, if they were the same P.H. he had changed a lot in eleven years. His round cheeks had caved in, his nose had shrunk, his lips were thinner, and his chin had bulged.

"No," Wolfe said. "Well?"

"Unanimous," I agreed. "That would have been a hell of a spot to find him. Is it worth going to the courtroom for a look?"

"I doubt it. Anyway, not today. You're needed here."

But that only postponed the agony for a few hours. That afternoon, after various journalists had been dealt with, and some of the P.H.'s, and Saul had been sent to keep the appointments, we had a visitor. Just three minutes after Wolfe had left the office for his daily four-to-six conference with the orchids, the doorbell rang and I answered it. On the stoop was a middle-aged guy who would need a shave by sundown, in a sloppy charcoal topcoat and a classy new black homburg. He could have been a P.H., but not a journalist. He said he would like a word with Mr. Nero Wolfe. I said Mr. Wolfe was engaged, told him my name and station, and asked if I could be of any service. He said he didn't know.

He looked at his wristwatch. "I haven't much time," he said, looking harassed. "My name is Albert Freyer, counselor-at-law." He took a leather case from his pocket, got a card from it, and handed it to me. "I am attorney for Peter Hays, who is on trial for first-degree murder. I'm keeping my cab waiting because the jury is out and I must be at hand. Do you know anything about the advertisement Nero Wolfe put in today's papers, 'To P.H.'?"

"Yes, I know all about it."

"I didn't see it until an hour ago. I didn't want to phone about it. I want to ask Nero Wolfe a question. It is being assumed that the advertisement was addressed to my client, Peter Hays. I want to ask him straight, was it?"

"I can answer that. It wasn't. Mr. Wolfe had never heard of Peter Hays, except in the newspaper accounts of his trial."

"You will vouch for that?"

"I do vouch for it."

"Well." He looked gotten. "I was hoping—No matter. Who is the P.H. the advertisement was addressed to?"

"A man whose initials are known to us but his name is not."

"What was the injustice mentioned in the ad? The wrong to be righted?"

"A theft that took place eleven years ago."

"I see." He looked at his wrist. "I have no time. I would like to give you a message for Mr. Wolfe. I admit the possibility of coincidence, but it is not unreasonable to suspect that it may be a publicity stunt. If so, it may work damage to my client, and it may be actionable. I'll want to look into the matter further when time permits. Will you tell him that?"

"Sure. If you can spare twenty seconds more, tell me something. Where was Peter Hays born, where did he spend his boyhood, and where did he go to college?"

Having half turned, he swiveled his head to me. "Why do you want to know?"

"I can stand it not to. Call it curiosity. I read the papers. I answered six questions for you, why not answer three for me?"

"Because I can't. I don't know." He was turning to go.

I persisted. "Do you mean that? You're defending him on a murder charge, and you don't know that much about him?" He was starting down the seven steps of the stoop. I asked his back, "Where's his family?"

He turned his head to say, "He has no family," and

went. He climbed into the waiting taxi and banged the door, and the taxi rolled away from the curb. I went back in, to the office, and buzzed the plant rooms on the house phone.

"Yes?" Wolfe hates to be disturbed up there.

"We had company. A lawyer named Albert Freyer. He's Peter Hays's attorney, and he doesn't know where Hays was born and brought up or what college he went to, and he says Hays has no family. I'm switching my vote. I think it's worth the trip, and the client will pay the cab fare. I'm leaving now."

"No."

"That's just a reflex. Yes."

"Very well. Tell Fritz."

The gook. I always did tell Fritz. I went to the kitchen and did so, returned to the office and put things away and locked the safe, fixed the phone to ring in the kitchen, and got my hat and coat from the rack in the hall. Fritz was there to put the chain bolt on the door.

After habits get automatic you're no longer aware of them. One day years ago a tail had picked me up when I left the house on an errand, without my knowing it, and what he learned from my movements during the next hour had cost us an extra week, and our client an extra several thousand dollars, solving a big and important case. For a couple of months after that experience I never went out on a business errand without making a point of checking my rear, and by that time it had become automatic, and I've done it ever since without thinking of it. That Tuesday afternoon, heading for Ninth Avenue, I suppose I glanced back when I had gone about fifty paces, since that's the routine, but if so I saw nothing. But in another fifty paces, when I glanced back again automatically, something clicked and shot to the upper level and I was aware of it. What had caused the click was the sight of a guy some forty yards behind, headed my way, who hadn't been there before. I stopped, turned, and stood, facing him. He hesitated, took a piece of paper from his pocket, peered at it, and started studying the fronts of houses to his right and left. Almost anything would have been better than that, even tying his shoestring, since his sudden appearance had to mean either that he had popped out of an areaway to follow me or that he had emerged from one of the houses on his own affairs; and if the latter, why stop to glom the numbers of the houses next door?

So I had a tail. But if I tackled him on the spot, with nothing but logic to go on, he would merely tell me to go soak my head. I could lead him into a situation where I would have more than logic, but that would take time, and Freyer had said the jury was out, and I was in a hurry. I decided I could spare a couple of minutes and stood and looked at him. He was middle-sized, in a tan raglan and a brown snap-brim, with a thin, narrow face and a pointed nose. At the end of the first minute he got embarrassed and mounted the stoop of the nearest house, which was the residence and office of Doc Vollmer, and pushed the button. The door was opened by Helen Grant, Doc's secretary. He exchanged a few words with her, turned away without touching his hat, descended to the sidewalk, mounted the stoop of the house next door, and pushed the button. My two minutes were up, and anyway that was enough, so I beat it to Ninth Avenue without bothering to look back, flagged a taxi, and told the driver Centre and Pearl Streets.

At that time of day the courthouse corridors were full of lawyers, clients, witnesses, jurors, friends, enemies, relatives, fixers, bloodsuckers, politicians, and citizens. Having consulted a city employee below, I left the elevator at the third floor and dodged my way down the hall and around a corner to Part XIX, expecting no difficulty about getting in, since the Hays case was no headliner, merely run-of-the-mill.

There certainly was no difficulty. The courtroom was practically empty—no judge, no jury, and even no clerk or stenographer. And no Peter Hays. Eight or nine people altogether were scattered around on the benches. I went and consulted the officer at the door, and was told that the jury was still out and he had no idea when it would be in. I found a phone booth and made two calls: one to Fritz, to tell him I might be home for dinner and I might not, and one to Doc Vollmer's number. Helen Grant answered.

"Listen, little blessing," I asked her, "do you love me?"

"No. And I never will."

"Good. I'm afraid to ask favors of girls who love me, and I want one from you. Fifty minutes ago a man in a tan coat rang your bell and you opened the door. What did he want?"

"My lord!" She was indignant. "Next thing you'll be tapping our phone! If you think you're going to drag me into one of your messes!"

"No mess and no dragging. Did he try to sell you some heroin?"

"He did not. He asked if a man named Arthur Holcomb lived here, and I said no, and he asked if I knew where he lived, and I said no again. That was all. What is this, Archie?"

"Nothing. Cross it off. I'll tell you when I see you if you still want to know. As for not loving me, you're just whistling in the dark. Tell me good-by."

"Good-by forever!"

So he had been a tail. A man looking for Arthur Holcomb wouldn't need to pop or slink suddenly from an areaway. There was no profit in guessing, but as I went back down the corridor naturally I wondered whether and how and why he was connected with P.H., and if so, which one.

As I approached the door of Part XIX I saw activity. People were going in. I got to the elbow of the officer and asked him if the jury was coming, and he said, "Don't ask me, mister. Word gets around fast here, but not to me. Move along." I entered the courtroom and stepped aside to be out of the traffic lane, and was surveying the scene when a voice at my shoulder pronounced my name. I turned, and there was Albert Freyer. His expression was not cordial.

"So you never heard of Peter Hays," he said through his teeth. "Well, you're going to hear of me."

My having no reply ready didn't matter, for he didn't wait for one. He walked down the center aisle with a companion, passed through the gate, and took a seat at the counselors' table. I followed and chose a spot in the third row on the left, the side where the defendant would enter.

The clerk and stenographer were at their desks, and Assistant District Attorney Mandelbaum, who had once been given a bigger dose by Wolfe than he could swallow, was at another table in the enclosure, with his briefcase in front of him and a junior at his side. People were straggling down the aisle, and I had my neck twisted for a look at them, with a vague idea of seeing the man in the tan coat who wanted to find Arthur Holcomb, when there was a sudden murmur and faces turned left, and so did mine. The defendant was being escorted in.

I have good eyes and I used them as he crossed to a chair directly behind Albert Freyer. I only had about four seconds, for when he was seated, with his back to me, my eyes were of no use, since the picture of Paul Herold, in mortarboard and gown, had given nothing to go by but the face. So I shut my eyes to concentrate. He was and he wasn't. He could be, but. Looking at the two pictures side by side with Wolfe, I would have made it thirty to one that he wasn't. Now two to one, or maybe even money, and I would take either end. I had to press down with my fanny to keep from bobbing up and marching through the gate for a full-face close-up.

The jury was filing in, but I hardly noticed. The courtroom preliminaries leading up to the moment when a jury is going to tell a man where he stands on the big one will give any spectator either a tingle in the spine or a lump of lead in his stomach, but not that time for me. My mind was occupied, and I was staring at the back of the defendant's head, trying to make him turn around. When the officer gave the order to rise for the entrance of the judge, the others were all on their feet before I came to. The judge sat and told us to do likewise, and we obeyed. I could tell you what the clerk said, and the question the judge asked the foreman, and the questions the clerk asked the foreman, since that is court routine, but I didn't actually hear it. I was back on my target.

The first words I actually heard came from the foreman. "We find the defendant guilty as charged, of murder in the first degree."

A noise went around, a mixture of gasps and murmurs, and a woman behind me tittered, or it sounded like it. I kept on my target, and it was well that I did. He rose and turned square around, all in one quick movement, and sent his eyes around the courtroom—searching, defiant eyes— and they flashed across me. Then the guard had his elbow and he was pulled around and down, and Albert Freyer got up to ask that the jury be polled.

At such a moment the audience is supposed to keep their seats and make no disturbance, but I had a call. Lowering my head and pressing my palm to my mouth as if I might or might not manage to hold it in, I got up and sidestepped to the aisle, and double-quicked to the rear and on out. Waiting for one of the slow-motion elevators didn't fit my mood, so I took to the stairs. Out on the sidewalk there were several citizens strung along on the lookout for taxis, so I went south a block, soon got one, climbed in, and gave the hackie the address.

The timing was close to perfect. It was 5:58 when, in response to my ring, Fritz came and released the chain bolt and let me in. In two minutes Wolfe would be down from the plant rooms. Fritz followed me to the office to report, the chief item being that Saul had phoned to say that he had seen the three P.H's and none of them was it. Wolfe entered, went to his desk, and sat, and Fritz left.

Wolfe looked up at me. "Well?"

"No sir," I said emphatically. "I am not well. I am under the impression that Paul Herold, alias Peter Hays, has just been convicted of first-degree murder."

His lips tightened. He released them. "How strong an impression? Sit down. You know I don't like to stretch my neck." ,

I went to my chair and swiveled to face him. "I was breaking it gently. It's not an impression, it's a fact. Do you want details?"

"Relevant ones, yes."

"Then the first one first. When I left here a tail picked me up. Also a fact, not an impression. I didn't have time to tease him along and corner him, so I passed it. He didn't follow me downtown—not that that matters."

Wolfe grunted. "Next."

"When I got to the courtroom the jury was still out,

but they soon came in. I was up front, in the third row. When the defendant was brought in he passed within twenty feet of me and I had a good look, but it was brief and it was mostly three-quarters and profile. I wasn't sure. I would have settled for tossing a coin. When he sat, his back was to me. But when the foreman announced the verdict he stood up and turned around to survey the audience, and what he was doing, or wanting to do, was to tell somebody to go to hell. I got his full face, and for that instant there was something in it, a kind of cocky something, that made it absolutely the face of that kid in the picture. Put a flattop and a kimono on him and take eleven years off, and he was Paul Herold. I got up and left. And by the way, another detail. That lawyer, Albert Freyer, I told him in effect that we weren't interested in Peter Hays, and he saw me in the courtroom and snarled at me and said we'd hear from him."

Wolfe sat and regarded me. He heaved a sigh. "Confound it. But our only engagement was to find him. Can we inform Mr. Herold that we have done so?"

"No. I'm sure, but not that sure. We tell him his son has been convicted of murder, and he comes from Omaha to take a look at him through the bars, and says no. That would be nice. Lieutenant Murphy expected to get a grin out of this, but that wouldn't be a grin, it would be a horse laugh. Not to mention what I would get from you. Nothing doing."

"Are you suggesting that we're stalemated?"

"Not at all. The best thing would be for you to see him and talk with him and decide it yourself, but since you refuse to run errands outside the house, and since he is in no condition to drop in for a chat, I suppose it's up to me —I mean the errand. Getting me in to him is your part."

He was frowning. "You have your gifts, Archie. I have always admired your resourcefulness when faced by barriers."

"Yeah, so have I. But I have my limitations, and this is it. I was considering it in the taxi on the way home. Cramer or Stebbins or Mandelbaum, or anyone else on the public payroll, would have to know what for, and they would tell Murphy and he would take over, and if he *is* Paul Herold, who would have found him? Murphy. It calls for better gifts than mine. Yours."

He grunted. He rang for beer. "Full report, please. All you saw and heard in the courtroom."

I obliged. That didn't take long. When I finished, with my emergency exit as the clerk was polling the jury, he asked for the *Times's* report of the trial, and I went to the cupboard and got it—all issues from March 27 to date. He started at the beginning, and, since I thought I might as well bone up on it myself, I started at the end and went backward. He had reached April 2, and I had worked back to April 4, and there would soon have been a collision but for an interruption. The doorbell rang. I went to the hall, and seeing, through the one-way glass panel of the front door, a sloppy charcoal topcoat and a black homburg that I had already seen twice that day, I recrossed the sill of the office and told Wolfe, "He kept his word. Albert Freyer."

His brows went up. "Let him in," he growled.

3

The counselor-at-law hadn't had a shave, but it must be admitted that the circumstances called for allowances. I suppose he thought he was flattening somebody when, convoyed to the office and introduced, he didn't extend a hand, but if so he was wrong. Wolfe is not a handshaker.

When Freyer had got lowered into the red leather chair Wolfe swiveled to face him and said affably, "Mr. Goodwin has told me about you, and about the adverse verdict on your client. Regrettable."

"Did he tell you you would hear from me?"

"Yes, he mentioned that."

"All right, here I am." Freyer wasn't appreciating the big, comfortable chair; he was using only the front half of it, his palms on his knees. "Goodwin told me your ad in today's papers had no connection with my client, Peter Hays. He said you had never heard of him. I didn't believe him. And less than an hour later he appears in the courtroom where my client was on trial. That certainly calls for an explanation, and I want it. I am convinced that my client is innocent. I am convinced that he is the victim of a diabolical frame-up. I don't say that your ad was a part of the plot, I admit I don't see how it could have been since it appeared on the day the case went to the jury, but I intend to—"

"Mr. Freyer." Wolfe was showing him a palm. "If you please. I can simplify this for you."

"You can't simplify it until you explain it to my satisfaction."

"I know that. That's why I am prepared to do something I have rarely done, and should never do except under compulsion. It is now compelled by extraordinary circumstances. I'm going to tell you what a client of mine has told me. Of course you're a member of the New York bar?"

"Certainly."

"And you are attorney-of-record for Peter Hays?"

"Yes."

"Then I'm going to tell you something in confidence."

Freyer's eyes narrowed. "I will not be bound in confidence in any matter affecting my client's interests."

"I wouldn't expect you to. The only bond will be your respect for another man's privacy. The interests of your client and my client may or may not intersect. If they do we'll consider the matter; if they don't, I shall rely on your discretion. This is the genesis of that advertisement."

He told him. He didn't report our long session with James R. Herold verbatim, but neither did he skimp it. When he was through, Freyer had a clear and complete picture of where we stood up to four o'clock that afternoon, when Freyer had rung our doorbell. The lawyer was a good listener and had interrupted only a couple of times, once to get a point straight and once to ask to see the picture of Paul Herold.

"Before I go on," Wolfe said, "I invite verification. Of course Mr. Goodwin's corroboration would have no validity for you, but you may inspect his transcription of the notes he made, five typewritten pages. Or you can phone Lieutenant Murphy, provided you don't tell him who you are. On that, of course, I am at your mercy. At this juncture I don't want him to start investigating a possible connection between your P.H. and my P.H."

"Verification can wait," Freyer conceded. "You would be a fool to invent such a tale, and I'm quite aware that you're not a fool." He had backed up in the chair and got more comfortable. "Finish it up."

"There's not much more. When you told Mr. Goodwin that your client's background was unknown to you and that he had no family, he decided he had better have a look at Peter Hays, and he went to the courtroom for that purpose. His first glimpse of him, when he was brought into court, left him uncertain; but when, upon hearing the verdict, your client rose and turned to face the crowd, his face had a quite different expression. It had, or Mr. Goodwin thought it had, an almost conclusive resemblence to the picture of the youthful Paul Herold. When you asked to see the picture, I asked you to wait. Now I ask you to look at it. Archie?"

I got one from the drawer and went and handed it to Freyer. He studied it a while, shut his eyes, opened them again, and studied it some more. "It could be," he conceded. "It could easily be." He looked at it some more. "Or it couldn't." He looked at me. "What was it about his face when he turned to look at the crowd?"

"There was life in it. There was—uh—spirit. As I told Mr. Wolfe, he was telling someone to go to hell, or ready to."

Freyer shook his head. "I've never seen him like that, with any life in him. The first time I saw him he said he might as well be dead. He had nothing but despair, and he never has had."

"I take it," Wolfe said, "that as far as you know he could be Paul Herold. You know nothing of his background or connections that precludes it?"

"No." The lawyer considered it. "No, I don't. He has refused to disclose his background, and he says he has no living relatives. That was one of the things against him with the District Attorney—not evidential, of course, but you know how that is."

Wolfe nodded. "Now, do you wish to verify my account?"

"No. I accept it. As I said, you're not a fool."

"Then let's consider the situation. I would like to ask two questions."

"Go ahead."

"Is your client in a position to pay adequately for your services?"

"No, he isn't. Adequately, no. That is no secret. I took the case at the request of a friend—the head of the advertising agency he works for—or worked for. All his associates at the agency like him and speak well of him, and so do others—all his friends and acquaintances I have had contact with. I could have had dozens of character witnesses if that would have helped any. But in addition to the prison bars he has erected his own barrier to shut the world out—even his best friends."

"Then if he is Paul Herold it seems desirable to establish that fact. My client is a man of substantial means. I am not trying to stir your cupidity, but the laborer is worthy of his hire. If you're convinced of your client's innocence you will want to appeal, and that's expensive. My second question: will you undertake to resolve our doubt? Will you find out, the sooner the better, whether your P.H. is my P.H.?"

"Well." Freyer put his elbows on the chair arms and flattened his palms together. "I don't know. He's a very difficult man. He wouldn't take the stand. I wanted him to, but he wouldn't. I don't know how I'd go about this. He would resent it, I'm sure of that, after the attitude he has taken to my questions about his background, and it might become impossible for me to continue to represent him." Abruptly he leaned forward and his eyes gleamed. "And I want to represent him! I'm convinced he was framed, and there's still a chance of proving it!"

"Then if you will permit a suggestion"—Wolfe was practically purring—"do you agree that it's desirable to learn if he is Paul Herold?"

"Certainly. You say your client is in Omaha?"

"Yes. He returned last night."

"Wire him to come back. When he comes tell him how it stands, and I'll arrange somehow for him to see my client."

Wolfe shook his head. "That won't do. If I find that it is his son who has been convicted of murder of course I'll have to tell him, but I will not tell him that it may be his son who has been convicted of murder and ask him to resolve the matter. If it is not his son, what am I? A bungler. But for my suggestion: if you'll arrange for Mr. Goodwin to see him and speak with him, that will do it."

"How?" The lawyer frowned. "Goodwin has already seen him."

"I said 'and speak with him.' " Wolfe turned. "Archie. How long would you need with him to give us a firm conclusion?"

"Alone?"

"Yes. I suppose a guard would be present."

"I don't mind guards. Five minutes might do it. Make it ten."

Wolfe went back to Freyer. "You don't know Mr. Goodwin, but I do. And he will manage it so that no resentment will bounce to you. He is remarkably adroit at drawing resentment to himself to divert it from me or one of my clients. You can tell the District Attorney that he is investigating some aspect of the case for you; and as for your client, you can safely leave that to Mr. Goodwin." He glanced up at the wall clock. "It could be done this evening. Now. I invite you to dine with me here. The sooner it's settled the better, both for you and for me."

But Freyer wouldn't buy that. His main objection was that it would be difficult to get access to his convicted client at that time of day even for himself, but also he wanted to think it over. It would have to wait until morning. When Wolfe sees that a point has to be conceded he manages not to be grumpy about it, and the conference ended much more sociably than it had begun. I went to the hall with Freyer and got his coat from the rack and helped him on with it, and let him out.

Back in the office, Wolfe was trying not to look smug. As I took the picture of Paul Herold from his desk to return it to the drawer, he remarked, "I confess his coming was opportune, but after your encounter with him in the courtroom it was to be expected."

"Uh-huh." I closed the drawer. "You planned it that way. Your gifts. It might backfire on you if his thinking it over includes a phone call to Omaha or even one to the Missing Persons Bureau. However, I admit you did the best you could, even inviting him to dinner. As you know, I have a date this evening, and now I can keep it."

So he dined alone, and I was only half an hour late joining the gathering at Lily Rowan's table at the Flamingo Club. We followed the usual routine, deciding after a couple of hours that the dance floor was too crowded and moving to Lily's penthouse, where we could do our own crowding. Getting home around three o'clock, I went to the office and switched a light on for a glance at my desk, where Wolfe leaves a note if there is something that needs early-morning attention, found it bare, and mounted the two flights to my room.

For me par in bed is eight full hours, but of course I have to make exceptions, and Wednesday morning I entered the kitchen at nine-thirty, only half awake but with my hair brushed and my clothes on, greeted Fritz with forced cheerfulness, got my orange juice, which I take at room temperature, from the table, and had just swallowed a gulp when the phone rang. I answered it there, and had Albert Freyer's voice in my ear. He said he had arranged it and I was to meet him in the City Prison visitors' room at ten-thirty. I said I wanted to be alone with his client, and he said he understood that but he had to be there to identify me and vouch for me.

I hung up and turned to Fritz. "I'm being pushed, damn it. Can I have two cakes in a hurry? Forget the sausage, just the cakes and honey and coffee."

He protested, but he moved. "It's a bad way to start a day, Archie, cramming your breakfast down."

I told him I was well aware of it and buzzed the plant rooms on the house phone to tell Wolfe.

4

I wasn't exactly alone. Ten feet to my right a woman sat on a wooden chair just like mine, staring through the holes of the steel lattice at a man on the other side. By bending an ear I could have caught what the man was saying, but I didn't try because I assumed she was as much in favor of privacy as I was. Ten feet to my left a man on another chair like mine was also staring through the lattice, at a lad who wasn't as old as Paul Herold had been when the picture was taken. I couldn't help hearing what he was saying, and apparently he didn't give a damn. The boy across the lattice from him was looking bored. There were three or four cops around, and the one who had brought me in was standing back near the wall, also looking bored.

During the formalities of getting passed in, which had been handled by Freyer, I had been told that I would be allowed fifteen minutes, and I was about to leave my chair to tell the cop that I hoped he wouldn't start timing me until the prisoner arrived, when a door opened in the wall on the other side of the lattice and there he was, with a guard behind his elbow. The guard steered him across to a chair opposite me and then backed up to the wall, some five paces. The convict sat on the edge of the chair and blinked through the holes at me.

"I don't know you," he said. "Who are you?"

At that moment, with his pale hollow cheeks and his dead eyes and his lips so thin he almost didn't have any, he looked a lot more than eleven years away from the kid in the flattop.

I hadn't decided how to open up because I do better if I wait until I have a man's face to choose words. I had a captive audience, of course, but that wouldn't help if he clammed up on me. I tried to get his eyes, but the damn lattice was in the way.

"My name is Goodwin," I told him. "Archie Goodwin. Have you ever heard of a private detective named Nero Wolfe?"

"Yes, I've heard of him. What do you want?" His voice was hollower than his cheeks and deader than his eyes.

"I work for Mr. Wolfe. Day before yesterday your father, James R. Herold, came to his office and hired him to find you. He said he had learned that you didn't steal that money eleven years ago, and he wanted to make it square with you. The way things stand that may not mean much to you, but there it is."

Considering the circumstances, he did pretty well. His jaw sagged for a second, but he jerked it up, and his voice was just the same when he said, "I don't know what you're talking about. My name is Peter Hays."

I nodded at him. "I knew you'd say that, of course. I'm sorry, Mr. Herold, but it won't work. The trouble is that Mr. Wolfe needs money, and he uses part of it to pay my salary. So we're going to inform your father that we have found you, and of course he'll be coming to see you. The reason I'm here, we thought it was only fair to let you know about it before he comes."

"I haven't got any father." His jaw was stiff now, and it affected his voice. "You're wrong. You've made a mistake. If he comes I won't see him!"

I shook my head. "Let's keep our voices down. What about the scar on your left leg on the inside of the knee? It's no go, Mr. Herold. Perhaps you can refuse to see your father—I don't know how much say they give a man in your situation—but he'll certainly come when we notify him. By the way, if we had had any doubt at all of your identity you have just settled it, the way you said if he comes you won't see him. Why should you get excited about it if he's not your father? If we've made a mistake the easiest way to prove it is to let him come and take a look at you. We didn't engage to persuade you to see him; our job was just to find you, and we've done that, and if—"

I stopped because he started to shake. I could have got up and left, since my mission was accomplished, but Freyer wouldn't like it if I put his client in a state of collapse and just walked out on him, and after all Freyer had got me in. So I stuck. There was a counter on both sides to keep us away from the lattice, and he had his fists on his, rubbing it with little jerks.

"Hang on," I told him. "I'm going. We thought you ought to know."

"Wait." He stopped shaking. "Will you wait?"

"Sure."

He took his fists off the counter, and his head thrust forward. "I can't see you very well. Listen to me, for God's sake. For God's sake don't tell him. You don't know what he's like."

"Well, I've met him."

"And my mother and sisters, they'll know. I think they believed I was framed on stealing that money, I think they believed me, but he didn't, and now I've been framed again. For God's sake don't tell him. This time it's all over, I'm going to die, and I might as well be dead now, and it's not fair for me to have this too. I don't want them to know. My God, don't you see how it is?"

"Yeah, I see how it is." I was wishing I had gone.

"Then promise me you won't tell him. You look like a decent guy. If I've got to die for something I didn't do, all right, I can't do anything about that, but not this too. I know I'm not saying this right, I know I'm not myself, but if you only—"

I didn't know why he stopped, because, listening to him, I didn't hear the cop approaching from behind. There was a tap on my shoulder, and the cop's voice.

"Time's up."

I arose.

"Promise me!" Paul Herold demanded.

"I can't," I told him, and turned and walked out.

Freyer was waiting for me in the visitors' room. I don't carry a mirror, so I don't know how my face looked when I joined him, but when we had left the building and were on the sidewalk, he asked, "It didn't work?"

"You can't always tell by my expression," I said. "Ask the people I play poker with. But if you don't mind I'll save it for Mr. Wolfe, since he pays my salary. Coming along?"

Evidently he was. I'll hand it to him that he could take a hint. In the taxi, when I turned my head to the window to study the scenery as we rolled along, he made no attempt to start a conversation. But he overdid it a little. When we stopped at the curb in front of the old brownstone, he spoke.

"If you want a word with Wolfe first I'll wait out here."

I laughed. "No, come on in and I'll find you some earmuffs."

I preceded him up the stoop and pushed the button, and Fritz let us in, and we put our hats and coats on the rack and went down the hall to the office. Wolfe, at his desk pouring beer, shot me a glance, greeted Freyer, and asked if he would like some beer. The lawyer declined and took the red leather chair without waiting for an invitation.

I stood and told Wolfe, "I saw him and talked with him. Instead of a yes or no, I'd like to give you a verbatim report. Do you want Mr. Freyer to hear it?"

Wolfe lifted his glass from the tray. "Is there any reason why he shouldn't?"

"No, sir."

"Then go ahead."

I didn't ham it, but I gave them all the words, which was no strain, since the only difference between me and a tape recorder is that a tape recorder can't lie. I lie to Wolfe only on matters that are none of his business, and this was his business. As I say, I didn't ham it, but I thought they ought to have a clear picture, so I described Paul Herold's condition—his stiff jaw, his shaking, his trying to shove his fists through the counter, and the look in his eyes when he said it wasn't fair for him to have this too. I admit one thing: I made the report standing up so I could put my fists on Wolfe's desk to show how Paul Herold's had looked on the counter. When I was through I slid the chair out from my desk and sat.

"If you still want a firm conclusion," I said, "it is yes."

Wolfe put his glass down, took in air clear to his belly button, and shut his eyes.

Freyer was shaking his head with his jaw set. "I've never had a case like it," he said, apparently to himself, "and I never want another one." He looked at Wolfe. "What are you going to do? You can't just shut your eyes on it."

"They're my eyes," Wolfe muttered, keeping them closed. In a moment he opened them. "Archie. That's why you wanted Mr. Freyer to hear your report, to make it even more difficult."

I lifted my shoulders and dropped them. "No argument."

"Then send Mr. Herold a telegram, saying merely that we have found his son, alive and well, here in New York. That was our job. Presumably he will come."

Freyer made a noise and came forward in his chair. I looked at Wolfe, swallowed, and spoke.

"You do it. I've got a sore finger. Just dial Western Union, WO two-seven-one-one-one."

He laughed. A stranger would have called it a snort, but I know his different snorts. He laughed some more.

"It's fairly funny," I said, "but have you heard the one about the centipede in the shoe store?"

Freyer said positively, "I think we should discuss it."

Wolfe nodded. "I agree. I was merely forcing Mr. Goodwin to reveal his position." He looked at me. "You prefer to wire Mr. Herold that I have decided I don't like the job?"

"If those are the only alternatives, yes. As he said, he might as well be dead. He's practically a corpse, and I don't have to rob corpses to eat and neither do you."

"Your presentment is faulty," Wolfe objected. "No robbery is contemplated. However, I am quite willing to consider other alternatives. The decision, of course, is mine. Mr. Herold gave me the job of finding his son, and it is wholly in my discretion whether to inform him that the job is done."

He stopped to drink some beer. Freyer said, "As the son's attorney, I have some voice in the matter."

Wolfe put the glass down and passed his tongue over his lips. "No, sir. Not on this specific question. However, though you have no voice you certainly have an interest, and it deserves to be weighed. We'll look at it f . Those two alternatives, telling my client that his son is found, or telling him that I withdraw from my job, call them A and B. If A, my surmise is that you would be through. He would come to see his son, and survey the situation, and decide whether to finance an appeal. If he decided no, that would end it. If he decided yes, he would probably also decide that you had mishandled the case and he would hire another lawyer. I base that on the impression I got of him. Archie?"

"Right." I was emphatic.

Wolfe returned to Freyer. "And if B, you'd be left where you are now. How much would an appeal cost?"

"That depends. A lot of investigation would be required. As a minimum, twenty thousand dollars. To fight it through to the end, using every expedient, a lot more."

"Your client can't furnish it?"

"No."

"Can you?"

"No."

"Then B is no better for you than A. Now what about me? A should be quite simple and satisfactory. I've done a job and I collect my fee. But not only must I pay my bills, I must also sustain my self-esteem. That man, your client, has been wounded in his very bowels, and to add insult to his injury as a mere mercenary would be a wanton act. I can't afford it. Even if I must gainsay Rochefoucauld, who wrote that we should only affect compassion, and carefully avoid having any."

He picked up his glass, emptied it, and put it down. "Won't you have some beer? Or something else?"

"No, thank you. I never drink before cocktail time."

"Coffee? Milk? Water?"

"No, thanks."

"Very well. As for B, I can't afford that either. I've done what I was hired to do, and I intend to be paid. And I have another reason for rejecting B. It would preclude my taking any further interest in this affair, and I don't like that. You said yesterday that you are convinced that your client is innocent. I can't say that I am likewise convinced, but I strongly suspect that you're right. With reason."

He paused because we were both staring and he loves to make people stare.

"With reason?" Freyer demanded. "What reason?"

Satisfied with the stares, he resumed. "When Mr. Goodwin left here yesterday afternoon to go to look at your client, a man followed him. Why? It's barely possible that it was someone bearing a grudge on account of some former activity of ours, but highly unlikely. It would be puerile for such a person merely to follow Mr. Goodwin when he left the house. He must be somehow connected with a present activtiy, and we are engaged in none at the moment except Mr. Herold's job. Was Mr. Herold checking on us? Absurd. The obvious probability is that my advertisement was responsible. Many people—newspapers, the police, you yourself—had assumed that it was directed at Peter Hays, and others might well have done so. One, let us say, named X. X wants to know why I declare Peter Hays to be innocent, but does not come, or phone, to ask me; and he wants to know what I am doing about it. What other devices he may have resorted to, I don't know; but one of them was to come, or send someone, to stand post near my house."

Wolfe turned a hand over. "How account for so intense and furtive a curiosity? If the murder for which Peter Hays was on trial was what it appeared to be—a simple and commonplace act of passion—who could be so inquisitive and also so stealthy? Then it wasn't so simple. You said yesterday that you were convinced that your client was the victim of a diabolical frame-up. If you're correct, no wonder a man was sent to watch my house when I announced, on the last day of his trial, that he was known to be innocent —as was assumed. And it is with reason that I suspect that there is someone, somewhere, who felt himself threatened by my announcement. That doesn't convince me that your client is innocent, but it poses a question that needs an answer."

Freyer turned to me. "Who followed you?"

I told him I didn't know, and told him why, and described the tail.

He said the description suggested no one to him and

went back to Wolfe. "Then you reject A and B for both of us. Is there a C?"

"I thnk there is," Wolfe declared. "You want to appeal. Can you take preliminary steps for an appeal without committing yourself to any substantial outlay for thirty days?"

"Yes. Easily."

"Very well. You want to appeal and I want to collect my fee. I warned my client that the search might take months. I shall tell him merely that I am working on his problem, as I shall be. You will give me all the information you have, all of it, and I'll investigate. In thirty days— much less, I hope—I'll know where we stand. If it is hopeless there will be nothing for it but A or B, and that decision can wait. If it is promising we'll proceed. If and when we get evidence that will clear your client, my client will be informed and he will foot the bill. Your client may not like it but he'll have to lump it; and anyway, I doubt if he would really rather die in the electric chair than face his father again, especially since he will be under no burden of guilt, either of theft or of murder. I make this proposal not as a paragon, but only as a procedure less repugnant than either A or B. Well, sir?"

The lawyer was squinting at him. "You say you'll investigate. Who will pay for that?"

"I will. That's the rub. I'll hope to get it back."

"But if you don't?"

"Then I don't."

"There should be a written agreement."

"There won't be. I take the risk of failure; you'll have to take the risk of my depravity." Wolfe's voice suddenly became a bellow. "Confound it, it is your client who has been convicted of murder, not mine!"

Freyer was startled, as well he might be. Wolfe can bellow. "I meant no offense," he said mildly. "I had no thought of depravity. As you say, the risk is yours. I accept your proposal. Now what?"

Wolfe glanced up at the wall clock and settled back in his chair. A full hour till lunchtime. "Now," he said, "I want all the facts. I've read the newspaper accounts, but I want them from you."

5

Peter Hays had been convicted of killing the husband of the woman he loved, on the evening of January 3, by shooting him in the side of the head, above the left ear, with a Marley .38. I might as well account for things as I go along, but I can't account for the Marley because it had been taken by a burglar from a house in Poughkeepsie in 1947 and hadn't been seen in public since. The prosecution hadn't explained how Peter Hays had got hold of it, so you can't expect me to.

The victim, Michael M. Molloy, forty-three, a real-estate broker, had lived with his wife, no children, in a four-room apartment on the top floor, the fifth, of a remodeled tenement on East 52nd Street. There was no other apartment on the floor. At 9:18 P.M. on January 3 a man had phoned police headquarters and said he had just heard a shot fired on one of the upper floors of the house next door. He gave the address of the house next door, 171 East 52nd Street, but hung up without giving his name, and he had never been located, though of course the adjoining houses had been canvassed. At 9:23 a cop from a prowl car had entered the building. When he got to the top floor, after trying two floors below and drawing blanks, he found the door standing open and entered. Two men were inside, one alive and one dead. The dead one, Molloy, was on the living-room floor. The live one, Peter Hays, with his hat and topcoat on, had apparently been about to leave, and when the cop had stopped him he had tried to tear away and had to be subdued. When he was under control the cop had frisked him and found the Marley .38 in his topcoat pocket.

All that had been in the papers. Also:

Peter Hays was a copywriter. He had been with the same advertising agency, one of the big ones, for eight years, and that was as far back as he went. His record and reputation were clean, with no high or low spots. Unmarried, he had lived for the past three years in an RBK—room, bath and kitchenette—on West 63rd Street. He played tennis, went to shows and movies, got along all right with people, had a canary in his room, owned five suits of clothes, four pairs of shoes, and three hats, and had no car. A key to the street door of 171 East 52nd Street had been found on his key ring. The remodeled building had a do-it-yourself elevator, and there was no doorman.

The District Attorney's office, the personnel of Homicide West, all the newspapers, and millions of citizens, were good and sore at Peter Hays because he wasn't playing the game. The DA and cops couldn't check his version of what had happened, and the papers couldn't have it analyzed by experts, and the citizens couldn't get into arguments about it, because he supplied no version. From the time he had been arrested until the verdict came, he had refused to supply anything at all. He had finally, urged by his lawyer, answered one question put by the DA in a private interview: had he shot Molloy? No. But why and when had he gone to the apartment? What were his relations with Molloy and with his wife? Why was a key to that building on his key ring? Why did he have the Marley .38 in his pocket? No reply. Nor to a thousand other questions.

Other people had been more chatty, some of them on the witness stand. The Molloys' daily maid had seen Mrs. Molloy and the defendant in close embrace on three different occasions during the past six months, but she had not told Mr. Molloy because she liked Mrs. Molloy and it was none of her business. Even so, Mr. Molloy must have been told something by somebody, or seen or heard something, because the maid had heard him telling her off and had seen him twisting her arm until she collapsed. A private detective, hired by Molloy late in November, had seen Mrs. Molloy and Peter Hays meet at a restaurant for lunch four times, but nothing juicier. There were others, but those were the outstanding items.

The prosecution's main attraction, though not its mainstay, had been the widow, Selma Molloy. She was twenty-nine, fourteen years younger than her husband, and was photogenic, judging from the pictures the papers had run. Her turn on the witness stand had sparked a debate. The Assistant DA had claimed the right to ask her certain questions because she was a hostile witness, and the judge had refused to allow the claim. For example, the ADA had tried to ask her, "Was Peter Hays your lover?" but he had to settle for "What were the relations between you and Peter Hays?"

She said she liked Peter Hays very much. She said she regarded him as a good friend, and she had affection for him, and believed he had affection for her. The relations between them could not properly be called misconduct. As for the relations between her and her husband, she had begun to feel less than a year after their marriage, which had taken place three years ago, that the marriage had been a mistake. She should have known it would be, since for a year before their marriage she had worked for Molloy as his secretary, and she should have known what kind of man he was. The prosecutor had fired at her, "Do you think he was the kind of man who should be murdered?" and Freyer had objected and been sustained, and the prosecutor had asked, "What kind of man was he?" Freyer had objected to that too as calling for an opinion on the part of the witness, and that had started another debate. It was brought out, specifically, that he had falsely accused her of infidelity, had physically mistreated her, had abused her in the presence of others, and had refused to let her get a divorce.

She had seen Peter Hays at a New Year's Eve party three days before the murder, and had not seen him since until she entered the courtroom that day. She had spoken with him on the telephone on January 1 and again on January 2, but she couldn't remember the details of the conversations, only that nothing noteworthy had been said. The evening of January 3 a woman friend had phoned around seven-thirty to say that she had an extra ticket for a show and invited her to come, and she had accepted. When she got home, around midnight, there were policemen in her apartment and she was told the news.

Freyer had not cross-examined her. One of the hundred or so details of privileged communications between a lawyer and a client furnished us by Freyer explained that. He had promised Peter Hays he wouldn't.

Wolfe snorted, not his laughing snort. "Isn't it," he inquired, "a function of counsel to determine the strategy and tactics of defense?"

"When he can, yes." Freyer, who had spent three-quarters of an hour reviewing the testimony and answering questions about it, had lubricated himself with a glass of water. "Not with this client. I've said he is difficult. Mrs. Molloy was the prosecution's last witness. I had five, and none of them helped any. Do you want to discuss them?"

"No." Wolfe looked at the wall clock. Twenty minutes to lunch. "I've read the newspaper accounts. I would like to know why you're convinced of his innocence."

"Well—it's a combination of things. His expressions, his tones of voice, his reactions to my questions and suggestions, some questions he has asked me—many things. But there was one specific thing. During my first talk with him, the day after he was arrested, I got the idea that he had refused to answer any of their questions because he wanted to protect Mrs. Molloy—either from being accused of the murder, or of complicity, or merely from harassment. At our second talk I got a little further with him. I told him that exchanges between a lawyer and his client were privilged and their disclosure could not be compelled, and that if he continued to withhold vital information from me I would have to retire from the case. He asked what would happen if I did retire and he engaged no other counsel, and I said the court would appoint counsel to defend him; that on a capital charge he would have to be represented by counsel. He asked if anything he told me would have to come out at the trial, and I said not without his consent."

The water glass had been refilled and he took a sip. "Then he told me some things, and more later. He said that on the evening of January third he had been in his apartment, alone, and had just turned on the radio for the nine-o'clock news when the phone rang. He answered it, and a man's voice said, 'Pete Hays? This is a friend. I just left the Molloys, and Mike was starting to beat her up. Do you hear me?' He said yes and started to ask a question, but the man hung up. He grabbed his hat and coat and ran, took a taxi across the park, used his key on the street door, took the elevator to the fifth floor, found the door of the Molloy apartment ajar, and went in. Molloy was lying there. He looked through the apartment and found no one. He went back to Molloy and decided he was dead. A gun was on a chair against the wall, fifteen feet from the body. He picked it up and put it in his pocket, and was looking around to see if there was anything else when he heard footsteps in the hall. He thought he would hide, then thought he wouldn't, and as he started for the door the policeman entered. That was his story. This is the first time anyone has heard it but me. I could have traced the cab, but why spend money on it? It could have happened just as he said, with only one difference, that Molloy was alive when he arrived."

Wolfe grunted. "Then I don't suppose that convinced you of his innocence."

"Certainly not. I'll come to that. To clean up as I go along: when I had him talking I asked why he had the key, and he said that on taking Mrs. Molloy home from the New Year's Eve party he had taken her key to open the door for her and had carelessly neglected to return it to her. Probably not true."

"Nor material. The problem is murder, not the devices of gallantry. What else?"

"I told him that it was obvious that he was deeply attached to Mrs. Molloy and was trying to protect her. His rushing to her on getting the anonymous phone call, his putting the gun in his pocket, his refusal to talk to the police, not only made that conclusive but also strongly indicated that he believed, or suspected, that she had killed her husband. He didn't admit it, but he didn't deny it, and for myself I was sure of it—provided he hadn't killed him himself. I told him that his refusal to divulge matters even to his attorney was understandable as long as he held that suspicion, but that now that Mrs. Molloy was definitely out of it I expected of him full and candid cooperation. She was completely in the clear, I said, because the woman and two men with whom she had attended the theater had stated that she had been with them constantly throughout the evening. I had a newspaper with me containing that news, and had him read it. He started to tremble, and the newspaper shook in his hands, and he called on God to bless me. I told him he needed God's blessing more than I did."

Freyer cleared his throat and took a gulp of water. "Then he read it again, more slowly, and his expression changed. He said that the woman and the men were old and close friends of Mrs. Molloy and would do anything for her. That if she had left the theater for part of the time they wouldn't hesitate to lie for her and say she hadn't. That there was no point in his spilling his guts—his phrase—unless it cleared him of the murder charge, and it probably wouldn't, and even if it did, then she would certainly be suspected and her alibi would be checked, and if it proved to be false she would be where he was then. I couldn't very well impeach his logic."

"No," Wolfe agreed.

"But I was convinced of his innocence. His almost hysterical relief on learning of her alibi, then the doubt creeping in, then his changing expression as he read the paper again and grasped the possibilities—if that was all counterfeit I should be disbarred for incompetence."

"Certainly I'm not competent to judge," Wolfe stated, "since I didn't see him. But since I have my own reason for not thinking it as simple as it seems I won't challenge yours. What else?"

"Nothing positive. Only negatives. I had to promise him I wouldn't cross-examine Mrs. Molloy, or quit the case, and I didn't want to quit. I had to accept his refusal to take the witness stand. If he had been framed the key question was the identity of the man who had made the phone call that made him dash to the Molloy apartment, but he said he had spent hours trying to connect the voice with someone he knew, and couldn't. The voice had been hoarse and guttural and presumably disguised, and he couldn't even guess.

"Two other negatives. He knew of no one who bore him enough ill will to frame him for murder, and he knew of no one who might have wanted Molloy out of the way. In fact he knows very little about Molloy—if he is to be believed, and I think he is. Of course the ideal suspect would be a man who coveted Mrs. Molloy and schemed to remove both her husband and Peter Hays at one stroke, but he is sure there is no such man. On those matters, and others, I have had no better luck with Mrs. Molloy."

"You have talked with her?"

"Three times. Once briefly and twice at length. She wanted me to arrange for her to see Peter, but he refused to permit it. She wouldn't tell me much about her relations with Peter, and there was no point in pressing her; I knew all I needed to know about that. I spent most of my time with her asking about her husband's activities and associates—everything about him. It had become apparent that I couldn't possibly get my client acquitted unless I found a likely candidate to replace him. She told me all she could, in fact she told me a lot, but there was a drag on her, and it wasn't hard to guess what the drag was. She thought Peter had killed her husband. The poor woman was pathetic; she kept asking me questions about the gun. It was obvious how her mind was working. She was willing to accept it that Peter had acted in a fit of passion, but if it had happened that way, how account for his having the gun with him? I asked her if there was any chance that the gun had been her husband's, there in the apartment, and she was sure there wasn't. When I told her that Peter had denied his guilt, and that I believed him, and why, she just stared at me. I asked her if she had in fact been continuously with her companions at the theater that evening, and she said yes, but her mind wasn't on that, it was on Peter. I honestly think she was trying to decide whether I really believed him or was only pretending to. As for what she told me about her husband, I didn't have the funds for a proper investigation—"

He stopped because Fritz had entered and was standing there. Fritz spoke. "Luncheon is ready, sir."

Wolfe got up. "If you'll join us, Mr. Freyer? There'll be enough to go around. Chicken livers and mushrooms in white wine. Rice cakes. Another place, Fritz."

6

At four o'clock that afternoon I left the house, bound for 171 East 52nd Street, to keep an appointment, made for me by Freyer, with Mrs. Michael M. Molloy.

After lunch we had returned to the office and taken up where we had left off. Freyer had phoned his office to send us the complete file on the case, and it had arrived and been pawed over. I had summoned Saul Panzer, Fred Durkin, Orrie Cather, and Johnny Keems to report to the office at six o'clock. They were our four main standbys, and they would call for a daily outlay of $160, not counting expenses. If it lasted a month, 30 times 160 equals 4800, so Wolfe's self-esteem might come high if he found he couldn't deliver.

Nothing had come of any of the leads suggested by what Mrs. Molloy had told Freyer about her deceased husband, and no wonder, since they had been investigated only by a clerk in Freyer's office and a sawbuck squirt supplied by the Harland Ide Detective Agency. I will concede that they had dug up some relevant facts: Molloy had had a two-room office in a twenty-story hive on 46th Street near Madison Avenue, and it said on the door MICHAEL M. MOLLOY, REAL ESTATE. His staff had consisted of a secretary and an errand boy. His rent had been paid for January, which was commendable, since January 1 had been a holiday and he had died on the third. If he had left a will, it had not turned up. He had been a fight fan and an ice-hockey fan. During the last six months of his life he had taken his current secretary, whose name was Delia Brandt, to dinner at a restaurant two or three times a week, but the clerk and the squirt hadn't got any deeper into that.

Mrs. Molloy hadn't been very helpful about his business affairs. She said that during her tenure as his secretary he had apparently transacted most of his business outside the office, and she had never known much about it. He had opened his own mail, which hadn't been heavy, and she had written only ten or twelve letters a week for him, and less than half of them had been on business matters. Her chief function had been to answer the phone and take messages when he was absent, and he had been absent most of the time. Apparently he had been interested almost exclusively in rural properties; as far as she knew, he had never had a hand in any New York City real-estate transactions. She had no idea what his income was, or his assets.

As for people who might have had a motive for killing him, she had supplied the names of four men with whom he had been on bad terms, and they had been looked into, but none of them seemed very promising. One of them had merely got sore because Molloy had refused to pay on a bet the terms of which had been disputed, and the others weren't much better. It had to be a guy who had not only croaked Molloy but had also gone to a lot of trouble to see that someone else got hooked for it, specifically Peter Hays, and that called for a real character.

In the taxi on my way uptown, if someone had hopped in and offered me ten to one that we had grabbed the short end of the stick, I would have passed. I will ride my luck on occasion, but I like to pick the occasion.

Number 171 East 52nd Street was an old walk-up which had had a thorough job of upgrading, inside and out, along with the houses on either side. They had all been painted an elegant gray, one with yellow trim, one with blue, and one with green. In the vestibule I pushed the button at the top of the row, marked MOLLOY, took the receiver from the hook and put it to my ear, and in a moment was asked who it was. I gave my name, and, when the latch clicked, pushed the door open, entered, and took the do-it-yourself elevator to the fifth floor. Emerging, I took a look around, noting where the stairs were. After all, this was the scene of the crime, and I was a detective. Hearing my name called, I turned. She was standing in the doorway.

She was only eight steps away, and by the time I reached her I had made a decision which sometimes, with one female or another, may take me hours or even days. I wanted no part of her. The reason I wanted no part was that just one look had made it plain that if I permitted myself to want a part it would be extremely difficult to keep from going on and wanting the whole; and that was highly inadvisable in the circumstances. For one thing, it wouldn't have been fair to P.H., handicapped as he was. This would have to be strictly business, not only outwardly but inwardly. I admit I smiled at her as she moved aside to let me enter, but it was merely a professional smile.

The room she led me into, after I put my coat and hat on a chair in the foyer, was a large and attractive living room with three windows. It was the room that P.H. had entered to find a corpse—if you're on our side. The rugs and furniture had been selected by her. Don't ask me how I know that; I was there and saw them, and saw her with them. She went to a chair over near a window, and, invited, I moved one around to face her. She said that Mr. Freyer had told her on the phone that he was consulting with Nero Wolfe, and that Mr. Wolfe wanted to send his assistant, Mr. Goodwin, to have a talk with her, and that was all she knew. She did not add, "What do you want?"

"I don't know exactly how to begin," I told her, "because we have different opinions on a very important point. Mr. Freyer and Mr. Wolfe and I all think Peter Hays didn't kill your husband, and you think he did."

She jerked her chin up. "Why do you say that?"

"Because there's no use beating around the bush. You think it because there's nothing else for you to think, and anyhow you're not really thinking. You've been hit so hard that you're too numb to think. We're not. Our minds are free and we're trying to use them. But we'd like to be sure on one point: if we prove we're right, if we get him cleared—I don't say it looks very hopeful, but if we do—would you like that or wouldn't you?"

"Oh!" she cried. Her jaw loosened. She said, "Oh," again, but it was only a whisper.

"I'll call that a yes," I said. "Then just forget our difference of opinion, because opinions don't count anyway. Mr. Freyer spent five hours with Nero Wolfe today, and Mr. Wolfe is going to try to find evidence that will clear Peter Hays. He has seen reports of your conversations with Freyer, but they didn't help any. Since you were Molloy's secretary for a year and his wife for three years, Mr. Wolfe thinks it likely—or, say, possible—that at some time you saw or heard something that would help. Remember he is assuming that someone else killed Molloy. He thinks it's very improbable that a situation existed which resulted in Molloy's murder, and that he never said or did anything in your presence that had a bearing on it."

She shook her head, not at me but at fate. "If he did," she said, "I didn't know it."

"Of course you didn't. If you had you would have told Freyer. Mr. Wolfe wants to try to dig it up. He couldn't ask you to come to his office so he could start the digging himself, because he has to spend two hours every afternoon playing with orchids, and at six o'clock he has a conference scheduled with four of his men who are going to be given other assignments—on this case. So he sent me to start in with you. I'll tell you how it works by giving you an example. Once I saw him spend eight hours questioning a young woman about everything and nothing. She wasn't suspected of anything; he was merely hoping to get some little fact that would give him a start. At the end of eight hours he got it: she had once seen a newspaper with a piece cut out of the front page. With that fact for a start, he got proof that a man had committed a murder. That's how it works. We'll start at the beginning, when you were Molloy's secretary, and I'll ask questions. We'll keep at it as long as you can stand it."

"It seems—" Her hand fluttered. I caught myself noticing how nice her hands were, and had to remind myself that that had all been decided. She said, "It seems so empty. I mean I'm empty."

"You're not really empty, you're full. When and where did you first meet Molloy?"

"That was four years ago," she said. "The way you—what you want to try—wouldn't it be better to start later? If there was a situation, the way you say, it would have been more recent, wouldn't it?"

"You never know, Mrs. Molloy." It seemed stiff to be calling her Mrs. Molloy. She fully deserved to be called Selma. "Anyhow, I have my instructions from Mr. Wolfe —and by the way, I skipped something. I was to tell you how simple it could have been. Say I decided to kill Molloy and frame Peter Hays for it. The drugstore on the corner is perfectly placed for me. Having learned that you are out for the evening and Molloy is alone in the apartment, at nine o'clock I phone Peter Hays from the booth in the drugstore and tell him—Freyer has told you what Peter says I told him. Then I cross the street to this house, am admitted by Molloy, shoot him, leave the gun here on a chair, knowing it can't be traced, go back down to the street, watch the entrance from a nearby spot until I see Hays arrive in a taxi and enter the building, return to the drugstore, and phone the police that a shot has just been fired on the top floor of One-seventy-one East Fifty-second Street. You couldn't ask for anything simpler than that."

She was squinting at me, concentrating. It gave the corners of her eyes a little upturn. "I see," she said. "Then your're not just—" She stopped.

"Just playing games? No. We really mean it. Settle back and relax a little. When and where did you first meet Molloy?"

She interlaced her fingers. No relaxing. "I wanted another job. I was modeling and didn't like it, and I knew shorthand. An agency sent me to his office, and he hired me."

"Had you ever heard of him before?"

"No."

"What did he pay you?"

"I started at sixty, and in about two months he raised it to seventy."

"When did he begin to show a personal interest in you?"

"Why—almost right away. The second week he asked me to have dinner with him. I didn't accept, and I liked the way he took it. He knew how to be nice when he wanted to. He always was nice to me until after we were married."

"Exactly what were your duties? I know what you told Freyer, but we're going to fill 'in."

"There weren't many duties, really—I mean there wasn't much work. I opened the office in the morning—usually he didn't come in until around eleven o'clock. I wrote his letters, but that didn't amount to much, and answered the phone, and did the filing, what there was of it. He opened the mail himself."

"Did you keep his books?"

"I don't think he had any books. I never saw any."

"Did you draw his checks?"

"I didn't at first, but later he asked me to sometimes."

"Where did he keep his checkbook?"

"In a drawer of his desk that he kept locked. There wasn't any safe in the office."

"Did you do any personal chores for him? Like getting prizefight tickets or buying neckties?"

"No. Or very seldom. He did things like that himself."

"Had he ever been married before?"

"No. He said he hadn't."

"Did you go to prizefights with him?"

"Sometimes I did, not often. I didn't like them. And later, the last two years, we didn't go places together much."

"Let's stick to the first year, while you were working for him. Were there many callers at the office?"

"Not many, no. Many days there weren't any."

"How many in an average week, would you say?"

"Perhaps—" She thought. "I don't know, perhaps eight or nine. Maybe a dozen."

"Take the first week you were there. You were new then and noticing things. How many callers were there the first week, and who were they?"

She opened her eyes at me. Wide open, they were quite different from when they were squinting. I merely noted that fact professionally. "But Mr. Goodwin," she said, "that's impossible. It was four years ago!"

I nodded. "That's just a warm-up. Before we're through you'll be remembering lots of things you would have thought impossible, and most of them will be irrelevant and immaterial. I hope not all of them. Try it. Callers the first week."

We kept at it for nearly two hours, and she did her best. She enjoyed none of it, and some of it was really painful, when we were on the latter part of the year, the period when she was cottoning to Molloy, or thought she was, and was making up her mind to marry him. She would have preferred to let the incidents of that period stay where they were, down in the cellar. I won't say it hurt me as much as it did her, since with me it was strictly business, but it was no picnic. Finally she said she didn't think she could go on, and I said we had barely started.

"Then tomorrow?" she asked. "I don't know why, but this seems to be tougher than it was with the police and the District Attorney. That seems strange, since they were enemies and you're a friend—you are a friend, aren't you?"

It was a trap, and I dodged it. "I want what you want," I told her.

"I know you do, but I just can't go on. Tomorrow?"

"Sure. Tomorrow morning. But I'll have some other errands, so it will have to be with Mr. Wolfe. Could you be at his office at eleven o'clock?"

"I suppose I could, but I'd rather go on with you."

"He's not so bad. If he growls just ignore it. He'll dig up something quicker than I would, in order to get rid of you. He doesn't appreciate women, and I do." I got out a card and handed it to her. "There's the address. Tomorrow at eleven?"

She said yes, and got up to see me to the door, but I told her that with a friend it wasn't necessary.

7

When I got back to 35th Street it was half-past six and the conference was in full swing.

I was pleased to see that Saul Panzer was in the red

leather chair. Unquestionably Johnny Keems had made a go for it, and Wolfe himself must have shooed him off. Johnny, who at one time, under delusions of grandeur, had decided my job would look better on him or he would look better on it, no matter which, but had found it necessary to abandon the idea, was a pretty good operative but had to be handled. Fred Durkin, big and burly and bald, knows exactly what he can expect of his brains and what he can't, which is more than you can say for a lot of people with a bigger supply. Orrie Cather is smart, both in action and in appearance. As for Saul Panzer, I thoroughly approve of his preference for free-lancing, since if he decided he wanted my job he would get it—or anybody else's.

Saul, as I say, was in the red leather chair, and the others had three of the yellow ones in a row facing Wolfe's desk. I got greetings and returned them, and circled around to my place. Wolfe remarked that he hadn't expected me so early.

"I tired her out," I told him. "Her heart was willing but her mind was weak. She'll be here at eleven in the morning. Do you want it now?"

"If you got anything promising."

"I don't know whether I did or not. We were at it nearly two hours, and mostly it was just stirring up the dust, but there were a couple of things, maybe three, that you might want to hear. One day in the fall of nineteen fifty-two, she thinks it was October, a man called at the office, and there was a row that developed into combat. She heard a crash and went in, and the caller was flat on the floor. Molloy told her he would handle it, and she returned to the other room, and pretty soon the caller came out on his feet and left. She doesn't know his name, and she didn't hear what the row was about because the door between the rooms was shut."

Wolfe grunted. "I hope we're not reduced to that. And?"

"This one was earlier. In the early summer. For a period of about two weeks a woman phoned the office nearly every day. If Molloy was out she left word for him to call Janet. If Molloy was in and took the call he told her he couldn't discuss the matter on the phone and rang off. Then the calls stopped and Janet was never heard from again."

"Does Mrs. Molloy know what she wanted to discuss?"

"No. She never listened in. She wouldn't."

He sent me a sharp glance. "Are you bewitched again?"

"Yes, sir. It took four seconds, even before she spoke. From now on you'll pay me but I'll really be working for her. I want her to be happy. When that's attended to I'll go off to some island and mope." Orrie Cather laughed, and Johnny Keems tittered. I ignored them and went on. "The third thing was in February or March nineteen-fifty-three, not long before they were married. Molloy phoned around noon and said he had expected to come to the office but couldn't make it. His ticket for a hockey game that night was in a drawer of his desk, and he asked her to get it and send it to him by messenger at a downtown restaurant. He said it was in a small blue envelope in the drawer. She went to the drawer and found the envelope, and noticed that it had been through the mail and slit open. Inside there were two things: the hockey ticket and a blue slip of paper, which she glanced at. It was a bill from the Metropolitan Safe Deposit Company for rent of a safe-deposit box, made out to Richard Randall. It caught her eye because she had once thought she might marry a man named Randall but had decided not to. She put it back in the envelope, which was addressed to Richard Randall, but if she noticed the address she has forgotten it. She had forgotten the whole incident until we dug it up."

"At least," Wolfe said, "if it's worth a question we know where to ask it. Anything else?"

"I don't think so. Unless you want the works."

"Not now." He turned to the others. "Now that you've heard Archie, you gentlemen are up to date. Have you any more questions?"

Johnny Keems cleared his throat. "One thing. I don't get the idea of Hays being innocent. I only know what I read in the papers, but it certainly didn't take the jury very long."

"You'll have to take that from me." Wolfe was brusque.

You have to be brusque with Johnny. He turned to me. "I've explained the situation to them in some detail, but I have not mentioned our client's name or the nature of his interest. We'll keep that to ourselves. Any more questions?"

There were none.

"Then we'll proceed to assignments. Archie, what about phone booths in the neighborhood?"

"The drugstore that Freyer mentioned is the nearest place with a booth. I didn't look around much."

He went to Durkin. "Fred, you will try that. The phone call to Peter Hays, at nine o'clock, was probably made from nearby, and the one to the police, at nine-eighteen, had to be made as quickly as possible after Peter Hays was seen entering the building. The hope is of course forlorn, since more than three months have passed, but you can try it. The drugstore seems the likeliest, but cover the neighborhood. If both phone calls were made from the same place, it's possible you can jog someone's memory. Start this evening, at once. The calls were made in the evening. Any questions?"

"No, sir. I've got it." Fred never takes his eyes off of Wolfe. I think he's expecting him to sprout either a horn or a halo, I'm not sure which, and doesn't want to miss it. "Shall I go now?"

"No, you might as well stay till we're through." Wolfe went to Cather. "Orrie, you will look into Molloy's business operations and associates and his financial standing. Mr. Freyer will see you at his office at ten in the morning. He'll give you whatever information he has, and you will start with that. Getting access to Molloy's records and papers will be rather complicated."

"If he kept books," I said, "they weren't in his office. At least Mrs. Molloy never saw them, and there was no safe."

"Indeed." Wolfe's brows went up. "A real-estate brokerage business and no books? I think, Archie, I'd better have a full report on the dust you stirred up." He returned to Orrie. "Since Molloy died intestate, as far as is known, his widow's rights are paramount in such matters as access to his records and papers, but they should be exercised as legal procedure provides. Mr. Freyer says that Mrs. Molloy has no attorney, and I'm going to suggest to her that she retain Mr. Parker. Mr. Freyer thinks it inadvisable to suggest him, and I agree. If Molloy kept no records in his office you will first have to find them. Any questions?"

Orrie shook his head. "Not now. I may have after I've talked with Freyer. If I do I'll phone you."

Wolfe made a face. Except in emergencies the boys never call between nine and eleven in the morning or four and six in the afternoon, when he is up in the plant rooms, but even so the damn phone rings when he's deep in a book or working a crossword or busy in the kitchen with Fritz, and he hates it. He went to Keems.

"Johnny, Archie will give you names and addresses. Mr. Thomas L. Irwin and Mr. and Mrs. Jerome Arkoff. They were Mrs. Molloy's companions at the theater; it was Mrs. Arkoff who phoned Mrs. Molloy that she had an extra ticket and invited her to join them. That may have no significance; X may merely have been awaiting an opportunity and grasped it; but he must have known that Mrs. Molloy would be out for the evening, and it is worth inquiry. Two investigators looked into it for Mr. Freyer, but they were extraordinarily clumsy, judging by their reports. If you get any hint that the invitation to Mrs. Molloy was designed, confer with me at once. I have known you to overstrain your talents."

"When?" Johnny demanded.

Wolfe shook his head. "Some other time. Will you communicate with me if you find cause for suspicion?"

"Sure. If you say so."

"I do say so." Wolfe turned to Saul Panzer. "For you, Saul, I had something in mind, but it can wait. It may be worth the trouble to learn why Molloy had in his possession an envelope addressed to Richard Randall, containing a bill for rental of a safe-deposit box, even though it was more than three years ago. If it were a simple matter to get information from the staff of a safe-deposit company about a customer I wouldn't waste you on it, but I know it isn't. Any questions?"

"Maybe a suggestion," Saul offered. "Archie might phone Lon Cohen at the *Gazette* and ask him to give me a good print of a picture of Molloy. That would be better than a newspaper reproduction."

The other three exchanged glances. They were all good operatives, and it would have been interesting to know, as a check on their talents, whether they had all caught the possibility as quickly as Saul had that Molloy had himself been Richard Randall. There was no point in asking them, since they would all have said yes.

"That will be done," Wolfe told him. "Anything else?"

"No, sir."

Wolfe came to me. "Archie. You've gone through Mr. Freyer's file and seen the report on Miss Delia Brandt, Molloy's secretary at the time of his death. You know where to find her."

"Right."

"Please do so. If she has anything we can use, get it. Since you are working for Mrs. Molloy you may need her approval. If so, get that."

Saul smiled. Orrie laughed. Johnny tittered. Fred grinned.

8

I joined Wolfe in the dining room at seven-fifteen as usual, and sat at table, but I didn't really dine because I had an eight-thirty date down in the Village and had to rush it some. Par for Wolfe from clams to cheese is an hour and a half.

Dating Delia Brandt hadn't been any strain on my talents. I had got her on the phone at the first try, given her my own name and occupation, and told her I had been asked by a client to see her and find out if she could supply enough material on Michael M. Molloy, her late employer, for a magazine article under her by-line, to be ghosted by the client. The proceeds would be split. After a few questions she said she would be willing to consider it and would be at home to me at eight-thirty. So I hurried a little with the roast duckling and left Wolfe alone with the salad.

It wouldn't have hurt the house at 43 Arbor Street any to get the same treatment as the one at 171 East 52nd. The outside could have used some paint, and a do-it-yourself elevator would have been a big improvement on the narrow, dingy wooden stairs. Three flights up, she was not waiting on the threshold to greet me, and, finding no button to push, I tapped on the door. From the time it took her you might have thought she had to traverse a spacious reception hall, but when the door opened the room was right there. I spoke.

"My name's Goodwin. I phoned."

"Oh," she said, "of course. I had forgotten. Come in."

It was one of those rooms that call for expert dodging to get anywhere. God knows why the piano bench was smack in the main traffic lane, and He also knows why there was a piano bench at all, since there was no piano. Anyway it was handy for my hat and coat. She crossed to a couch and invited me to sit, and since there was no chair nearby I perched on the couch too, twisting around to face her.

"I really had forgotten," she said apologetically. "My mind must have been soaring around." She waved a hand to show how a mind soars.

She was young, well shaped and well kept, well dressed and well shod, with a soft, clear skin and bright brown eyes, and well-cut fine brown hair, but a mind that soared. . . .

"Didn't you say you were a detective?" she asked. "Something about a magazine?"

"That's right," I told her. "This editor thinks he'd like to try a new slant on a murder. There have been thousands of pieces about murderers. He thinks he might use one called 'The Last Month of a Murdered Man' or 'The Last Year of a Murdered Man.' By his secretary."

"Oh, not my name?"

"Sure, your name too. And, now that I've seen you, a good big picture of you. I wouldn't mind having one myself."

"Now don't get personal."

It was hard to believe, the contrast between what my eyes saw and my ears heard. Any man would have been glad to walk down a theater aisle with her, but there would have to be an understanding that she would keep her mouth shut.

"I'll try not to," I assured her. "I can always turn my back. The idea is this: you'll tell me things about Mr. Molloy, what he said and did and how he acted, and I'll report to the editor, and if he thinks there's an article in it he'll come and talk with you. How's that?"

"Well, it couldn't be called 'The Last Year of a Murdered Man.' It would have to be called 'The Last Ten Months of a Murdered Man' because I only worked for him ten months."

"Okay, that's even better. Now. I understand—"

"How many days are there in ten months?"

"It depends on the months. Roughly three hundred."

"We could call it. 'The Last Three Hundred Days of a Murdered Man.' "

"A good idea. I understand that occasionally you had dinner with Molloy at a restaurant. Was it—"

"Who told you that?"

I had three choices: get up and go, strangle her, or sit on her. "Look, Miss Brandt. I'm being paid by the hour and I've got to earn it. Was it to discuss business matters or was it social?"

She smiled, which made her even prettier. "Oh, that was just social. He never talked about business to me. It had got so he didn't want to have dinner with his wife, and he hated to eat alone. I'd love to put that in. I know some people think I allowed him liberties, but I never did."

"Did the try to take liberties?"

"Oh, of course. Married men always do. That's because with their wives it's not a liberty any more."

"Yeah, that's why I've never married. Did he—"

"Oh, aren't you married?"

But you've had enough of her. So had I, but I was on duty, and I stuck with it for three solid hours. I had to go through another ordeal, about halfway through. We were thirsty, and she went to the kitchenette for liquid, and came back with a bottle of ginger ale, a bottle of gin, and two glasses with one cube of ice in each. I apologized, said I had ulcers, and asked for milk. She said she didn't have any, and I asked for water. I will go beyond the call of duty in a pinch, but I wouldn't drink gin and ginger ale to get the lowdown on Lizzie Borden. It was bad enough to sit there and watch her sipping away at it.

In the taxi on my way downtown to keep the date, I had felt some slight compunction at imposing on a poor working girl with a phony approach. In the taxi on my way home, having told her I would let her know if the editor still liked the idea, my conscience was sound asleep. If a conscience could snore, it probably would have.

Wolfe, who rarely turns in before midnight, was at his desk, reading *A Secret Understanding* by Merle Miller. He didn't look up when I entered, so I went to the safe for the expense book and entered the amounts I had given the hired help for expenses, a hundred bucks for each, put the book back and closed the safe and locked it, and cleared up my desk. I refuse to meet a cluttered desk in the morning.

Then I stood and looked down at him. "Excuse me. Anything from Fred or Johnny that needs attention?"

He finished a paragraph and looked up. "No. Fred called at eleven and reported no progress. Johnny didn't call."

"Shall I save mine for morning?"

"No. That woman will be here. Did you get anything?"

"I don't know." I sat. "She's either a featherbrain or a damn good imitation. She starts every other sentence with 'Oh.' You'd walk out on her in three minutes. She drinks four parts ginger ale and one part gin."

"No."

"Yes."

"Good heavens. Did you?"

"No. But I had to watch her. Two items. One day last October a button on his coat was loose and she offered to sew it on for him. While she was doing so some papers fell out of the pocket and when she picked them up she glanced at them. So she says; papers can fall out of pockets or they can be taken out. Anyhow, she was looking at one of the papers which was a list of names and figures when he suddenly entered from his room, snatched the paper from her, and gave her hell. He slapped her, but that's off the record because she doesn't want it to be in the article, and besides he apologized and bought her champagne at dinner that evening. She says he was so mad he turned white."

"And the names and figures?"

"I hoped you would ask that. She can't remember. She thinks the figures were amounts of money, but she's not sure."

"Hardly a bonanza."

"No, sir. Neither is the other item, but it's more recent. One day between Christmas and New Year's he asked her how she would like to take a trip to South America with him. He had to go on business and would need a secretary. I should mention that he had been trying to take liberties and she hadn't allowed it. She liked the idea of a trip to South America, but, knowing that what are liberties up here are just a matter of course down there, she told him she'd think it over. He said there wouldn't be much time for thinking it over because the business matters wouldn't wait. He also said they were confidential matters and made her promise she wouldn't mention the proposed trip to anyone. She put him off and hadn't said yes or no by January third, the day he died. So she says. I think she said yes. She is not a good liar. I didn't mention that her mind soars."

"Soars where?"

I waved a hand. "Just soars. You would enjoy her."

"No doubt." He looked up at the clock. Past midnight. "Has she a job?"

"Oh, yes. With an import firm downtown. Apparently no connection."

"Very well." He pushed his chair back, yawned, and got up. "Johnny should have reported. Confound him, he's too set on a master stroke."

"Instructions for morning?"

"No. I'll need you here for developments. If any. Good night."

He went, to the elevator, and I went, to the stairs. Up in my room, undressing, I decided to dream of Selma

Molloy—something like her being trapped in a blazing building, at an upper window, afraid to jump for the firemen's net. I would march up, wave the firemen aside, stretch my arms, and down she would come, light as a feather, into my embrace. The light as a feather part was important, since otherwise there might have been some bones broken. I didn't consider this reneging on my decision, because you can't hold a man responsible for his dreams. But I didn't follow through on it. No dreams at all. In the morning I didn't even remember that I had been going to dream, but I never do remember anything in the morning until I have washed and showered and shaved and dressed and made my way down to the kitchen. With the orange juice the fog begins to lift, and with the coffee it's all clear. It's a good thing Wolfe breakfasts in his room, on a tray taken up by Fritz, and then goes up to the plant rooms. If we met before breakfast he would have fired me or I would have quit long ago.

Thursday started busy and kept it up. There were three letters from P.H.'s, answers to the ad, in the morning mail, and I had to answer them. There was a phone call from Omaha, from James R. Herold. His wife was impatient. I told him we had five men working on the case, including Saul Panzer and me, and we would report as soon as there was anything worth reporting. Fred Durkin came in person to confer. He had visited five establishments with phone booths within two blocks of the 52nd Street house, and had found no one who remembered anything about any user of the phone around nine o'clock on January 3. The soda jerk who had been on duty at the drugstore that evening had left and gone somewhere in Jersey. Should Fred find him? I told him yes and wished him luck.

Orrie Cather phoned from Freyer's office to ask if we had arranged with Mrs. Molloy to hire a lawyer to establish her position legally, and I told him no, that would be done when she came to see Wolfe.

Lon Cohen of the *Gazette* phoned and said he had a riddle for me. It goes like this, he said. "Archie Goodwin tells me on Tuesday that he and Nero Wolfe aren't interested in the Hays murder trial. The P.H. in Wolfe's ad is a different person, no connection. But Wednesday evening

I get a note from Goodwin asking me to give the bearer,
Saul Panzer, a good clear print of a picture of Michael M.
Molloy. Here's the riddle: what's the difference between
Archie Goodwin and a double-breasted liar?"

I couldn't blame him, but neither could I straighten him
out. I told him the note Saul had brought him must have
been a forgery, and promised to give him a front-page
spread as soon as we had one.

Selma Molloy came on the dot at eleven. I let her in
and took her coat, a quiet gray plaid, in the hall, and was
putting it on a hanger when the elevator bumped to a
stop and Wolfe emerged. He stopped, facing her, inclined
his head nearly an inch when I pronounced her name,
turned, and made for the office, and I convoyed her in and
to the red leather chair. He sat and leveled his eyes at
her, trying not to scowl. He hates to work, and this would
probably be not only an all-day session, but all day with a
woman. Then he had an idea. His head turned and he
spoke.

"Archie. Since I'm a stranger to Mrs. Molloy, and you
are not, it might be better for you to tell her about the
legal situation regarding her husband's estate."

She looked at me. In her apartment she had sat with
her back to a window, and here she was facing one, but
the stronger light gave me no reason to lower my guard.

She squinted at me. "His estate? I thought you wanted
to go on from yesterday."

"We do," I assured her. "By the way, I told you I
wouldn't be here, but my program was changed. The
estate thing is a part of the investigation. We want access to Molloy's records and papers, and since no will has
been found the widow has a right to them, and you're the
widow. Of course you can let us look at anything that's in
the apartment, but there should be some legal steps—for
instance, you should be named as administrator."

"But I don't want to be administrator. I don't want
anything to do with his estate. I might have wanted some
of the furniture, if—" She let it hang. She shook her
head. "I don't want anything."

"What about cash for your current expenses?"

"I wondered about that yesterday, after you had gone."

Her eyes were meeting mine, straight. "Whether Nero Wolfe was expecting me to pay him."

"He isn't." I looked at Wolfe, and his head moved left, just perceptibly, and back. So we were still keeping our client under our hat. I met her eyes again. "Our interest in the case developed through a conversation with Mr. Freyer, and all we expect from you is information. I asked about cash only because there must be some in your husband's estate."

"If there is I don't want it. I have some savings of my own, enough to go along on a while. I just don't know what I'm going to do." She pinned her lower lip with her teeth, and after a moment released it. "I don't know what I'm going to do, but I don't want to be administrator or have anything to do with it. I should have left him long ago, but I had married him with my eyes open and my silly pride—"

"Okay, but it might help if we could take a look at his papers. For instance, his checkbook. Miss Brandt tells me that the furniture in the office was sold, and that before it was taken away some man went through the desks and removed the contents. Do you know about that?"

"Yes, that was a friend of mine—and he had been a friend of my husband's—Tom Irwin. He said the office should be closed up and I asked him to attend to it."

"What happened to the stuff he took?"

"He brought it to the apartment. It's there now, in three cartons. I've never looked at it."

"I would like to. You'll be here with Mr. Wolfe for quite a while. I could go up to the apartment and do it now if you're willing to let me have the key."

Without the slightest hesitation she said, "Of course," and opened her handbag. It didn't put her down a notch in my book—her being so trustful with a comparative stranger. All it meant was that with her P.H. convicted of murder she didn't give a damn about anything at all, and besides, I was the comparative stranger. Glancing at Wolfe and getting a nod, I went to her and took the keys, told her I would let her know if I found anything helpful and would give her a receipt for anything I brought away, and headed for the hall. I had just taken my topcoat from the rack when the doorbell rang, and a look through the one-way glass panel showed me Saul Panzer out on the stoop. Putting the coat back, I opened up.

There are things about Saul I don't understand and never will. For instance, the old cap he always wears. If I wore that cap while tailing a subject I'd be spotted in the first block. If I wore it while calling on people for information they would suspect I was cuckoo or quaint and draw the curtains. But Saul never gets spotted unless he wants to, and for extracting material from people's insides nothing can equal him except a stomach pump. While he was hanging up his coat and sticking the cap in its pocket I stepped to the office door to tell Wolfe, and Wolfe said to bring him in. He came, and I followed him.

"Yes?" Wolfe inquired.

Saul, standing, shot a glance at the red leather chair and said, "A report."

"Go ahead. Mrs. Molloy's interest runs with ours. Mrs. Molloy, this is Mr. Panzer."

She asked him how he did and he bowed. That's another thing about him, his bow; it's as bad as his cap. He sat down on the nearest yellow chair, knowing that Wolfe wants people at eye level, and reported.

"Two employees of the Metropolitan Safe Deposit Company identified a picture of Michael M. Molloy. They say it's a picture of Richard Randall, a renter of a box there. I didn't tell them it was Molloy, but I think one of them suspects it. I didn't try to find out what size the box is or when he first rented it or any other details, because I thought I'd better get instructions. If they get stirred up enough to look into it and decide that one of their boxes was probably rented under another name by a man who has been murdered, they'll notify the District Attorney. I don't know the law, I don't know what rights the DA has after he has got a conviction, since he couldn't be looking for evidence, but I thought you might want to get to the box first."

"I do," Wolfe declared. "How good is the identification?"

"I'd bank on it. I'm satisfied. Do you want to know just how it went?"

"No. Not if you're satisfied. How much are they already stirred up?"

"I think not much. I was pretty careful. I doubt if either of them will go upstairs with it, but they might, and I thought you might want to move."

"I do." Wolfe turned. "Mrs. Molloy. Do you know what this is about?"

"Yes, I think so." She looked at me. "Isn't it what I told you yesterday, the envelope and slip of paper when I was looking for the hockey ticket?"

"That's it," I told her.

"And you've found out already that my husband was Richard Randall?"

"We have," Wolfe said, "and that changes the situation. We must find out what is in that box as soon as possible, and to do so we must, first, demonstrate that Randall was Molloy, and, second, establish your right to access. Since in handling his safe-deposit box a man certainly makes fingerprints, the first presents no technical problem, but it must wait upon the second. When you said, madam, that you would have nothing to do with your husband's estate, I understood and respected your attitude. Rationally it could not be defended, but emotionally it was formidable; and when feeling takes over sense is impotent. Now it's different. We must see the contents of that box, and we can get to it only through you. You will have to assert your rights as the widow and take control of the estate. The law can crawl and usually does, but in an emergency it can—What are you shaking your head for?"

"I've told you. I won't do that."

Hearing her tone, and seeing her eyes and her jaw, he started to glare but decided it wouldn't work. So he turned to me. "Archie."

I did the glaring, at him, and then toned the glare down as I transferred it to her. "Mrs. Molloy," I said, "Mr. Wolfe is a genius, but geniuses have their weak spots, and one of his is that he pretends to believe that attractive young women can refuse me nothing. It comes in handy when an attractive young woman says no to something he wants, because it's an excuse for passing the buck to me, which he just did. I don't know what to do with it and he can't expect me to—he just said himself that when feeling takes over sense is impotent, so what good will it do to try to reason with you? But may I ask you a question?"

She said yes.

"Suppose no good grounds for a retrial or an appeal are found, and the sentence is carried out, and Peter Hays dies in the electric chair, and some time later, when a court gets around to it, that safe-deposit box is opened and it contains something that starts an investigation and leads to evidence that someone else committed the murder. What would your feeling be then?"

She had her lip pinned again, and had to release it to say, "I don't think that's a fair question."

"Why not? All I did was suppose, and it wasn't inconceivable. That box may be empty, but it could contain what I said. I think the trouble is that you don't believe there is any evidence, in that safe-deposit box or anywhere else, that will clear Peter Hays, beceuse he's guilty, so why should you do something you don't want to do?"

"That's not true! It's not true!"

"You know damn well it's true."

Her head went down, forward, and her hands came up to cover her face. Wolfe glowered at me. From that room he has walked out on a lot of different people, but when a woman goes to pieces he doesn't walk out, he runs. I shook my head at him. I didn't think Selma Molloy was going to slip the bit.

She didn't. When she finally raised her head her eyes met mine and she said calmly, "Listen, Mr. Goodwin. Didn't I help all I could yesterday and didn't I come today? You know I did. But how can I claim any rights as Mike Molloy's widow when for two years I bitterly regretted I was his wife? Don't you see it's impossible? Isn't there some other way? Can't I ask for someone else to be administrator and he can have rights?"

"I don't know," I told her. "That's a legal question."

"Get Mr. Parker," Wolfe snapped.

I turned and pulled the phone to me and dialed. Since Nathaniel Parker had answered some ten thousand legal questions for us over the years I didn't have to look up the number. While I was getting him Saul Panzer asked Wolfe if he should leave, and was told to wait until there was some place for him to leave for. When I had Parker, Wolfe took his phone.

I had to admire his performance. He would have liked to tell Parker that we were being obstructed by a perverse and capricious female, but with her sitting there that would have been inadvisable, so he merely said that for reasons of her own the widow refused to assert her claims, and put the legal problem. From there on his part was mostly grunts.

When he hung up he turned to the female. "Mr. Parker says it's complicated, and since it's urgent he wants to ask you some questions. He will be here in twenty minutes. He says it will expedite matters if you will decide whom you would like to suggest as administrator. Have you anyone in mind?"

"Why—no." She frowned. She looked at me, and back at him. "Could it be Mr. Goodwin?"

"My dear madam." Wolfe was exasperated. "Use your faculties. You met Mr. Goodwin yesterday for the first time, in his capacity as a private investigator. It would be highly inappropriate, and the court would find it so. It should be someone you know well, and trust. What about the man who closed the office and took the cartons to your apartment? Thomas Irwin."

"I don't think—" She considered it. "I don't think I'd want to ask him to do this. His wife wouldn't like it. But I wouldn't mind asking Pat Degan. He might say no, but I could ask him."

"Who is he?"

"Patrick A. Degan. He's the head of the Mechanics Alliance Welfare Association. His office isn't far from here, on Thirty-ninth Street. I could call him now."

"How long have you known him?"

"Three years, since I was married. He was a friend of

my husband's, but he always—I mean, he really is my
my friend, I'm sure he is. Shall I call him? What will I
say?"

"Tell him you wish to request a favor of him, and
ask him to come here. Now, if possible. If he asks questions tell him you would rather not discuss it on the
phone. And I venture a suggestion, in case he comes and
consents to act. Legal services will be required, and he
may want to name the lawyer to be engaged to per-
form them. I urge you not to agree. From a legal stand-
point it will be your interests the lawyer will represent,
whether you wish to renounce them or not, and it will
be proper and desirable for you to choose him."

"Why can't I choose the lawyer he names?"

"Because I wouldn't trust him. Because I suspect Mr.
Degan of having killed your husband."

She goggled at him. "You suspect Pat Degan? You
never heard of him until just now!"

Wolfe nodded. "I made it sensational. Purposely. I suspect each and all of your husband's associates, as I must
until I have reason to discriminate, and Mr. Degan is one
of them. I advise you not to let him name the lawyer.
If you are at a loss to choose one, I suggest Nathaniel
Parker, who will be here shortly. I have dealt with him
many years, and I recommend him without reservation.
As for trusting me, either you believe that I am earnestly
seeking an end you desire or it is folly for you to be here
at all."

It was a good pitch, but it didn't do the job—not completely. She looked at me, looking the question instead of
asking it.

I gave her a strictly professional smile. "Parker is as good
as they come, Mrs. Molloy."

"All right, then." She arose. "May I use the phone?"

9

Since Patrick A. Degan was the first suspect we had laid eyes on, unless you want to count Albert Freyer or Delia Brandt, naturally I gave him some attention, and I had plenty of opportunity during the hour that the conference lasted. In appearance I wouldn't have called him sinister—a medium-sized specimen in his early forties with a fair start on a paunch, round face, wide nose, and dark brown eyes that moved quickly and often. He greeted Selma Molloy as a friend, taking her hand in both of his, but not as one who had been bewitched by her into shooting her husband and framing her P.H. for it. I had him mostly in profile during the conference, since he was on a yellow chair facing Wolfe, with Nathaniel Parker on another one between Degan and me. After making the phone call, Mrs. Molloy had returned to the red leather chair. Saul Panzer had retired to one in the rear, over by the bookshelves.

When the situation had been explained to Degan by Mrs. Molloy and she had asked the favor, he wasted five minutes trying to get her to change her mind. When he saw that was no go, he said he would be willing to do what she wanted provided it was legally feasible, and on that point he would have to consult his lawyer. She said of course he would want to ask his lawyer about it, but her lawyer, Mr. Parker, was right there and would explain how it could be done. Not bad for a girl who wasn't using her faculties. Degan turned his quick brown eyes on Parker, polite but not enthusiastic. Parker cleared his throat and started in. That was the first he had heard that he was Mrs. Molloy's counsel, since he had had only a minute or two with us before Degan arrived, but he didn't raise the point.

From there on it got highly technical, and I had a notion, rejected as unprofessional, to give Mrs. Molloy's faculties a recess by taking her up to the plant rooms and showing her the orchids. Anyone sufficiently interested can call Parker at his office, Phoenix 5-2382, and get the details. What it boiled down to was that there were three different ways of handling it, but one would be much too slow, and which of the other two was preferable? Degan made two phone calls to his lawyer, and finally they got it settled. Parker would start the ball rolling immediately, and Degan agreed to be available for an appearance before a judge on short notice. Parker thought we might get a look at the inside of the safe-deposit box by Monday, and possibly sooner. He was just getting up to go when the phone rang and I answered it.

It was Sergeant Purley Stebbins of Homicide West. He told me some news, and I asked a few questions, and when he asked me a question I decided I didn't know the answer and asked him to hold the wire. Covering the transmitter, I turned to Wolfe.

"Stebbins. At eleven-forty-eight last night a man was hit by a car on Riverside Drive in the Nineties, and killed. The body has been identified as that of John Joseph Keems. About an hour ago the car that hit him was found parked on upper Broadway, and it's hot. It was stolen last night from where it was parked on Ninety-second Street. The fact that it was a stolen car makes Purley think it may have been premeditated murder, possibly in connection with a case Keems was working on, and, knowing that Johnny Keems often does jobs for you, he asks if he was working for you last night. I told him you sometimes hire an operative without telling me, and I'd ask you. I'm asking you."

"Tell him I'm engaged and you'll call him back."

I did so, hung up, and swiveled. Wolfe's lips were tight, his eyes were half closed, and his temple was twitching. He met my eyes and demanded, "You knew him. How much chance is there that he would have let a car kill him by inadvertence?"

"Practically none. Not Johnny Keems."

Wolfe's head turned. "Saul?"

"No, sir." Saul had got to his feet while I was reporting

to Wolfe. "Of course it could happen, but I agree with Archie."

Wolfe's head turned more, to the left. "Mrs. Molloy, if Mr. Goodwin was correct when he said that you believe there can be no evidence that will clear Peter Hays, this bitter pill for me is not so bitter for you. Not only can there be such evidence, there will be. Johnny Keems was working for me last night, on this case, and he was murdered. That settles it. You have been told that I thought it likely that Peter Hays is innocent; now I know he is."

His head jerked right. "Mr. Parker, the urgency is now pressing. I beg you to move with all possible speed. Well?"

I wouldn't say that Parker moved with all possible speed, but he moved. He made for the hall and was gone.

Degan, lifted from his chair by Wolfe's tone and manner, had a question. "Do you realize what you're saying?"

"Yes, sir, I do. Why? Do you challenge it?"

"No, I don't challenge it, but you're worked up and I wondered if you realized that you were practically promising Mrs. Molloy that Peter Hays will be cleared. What if you're giving her false hopes? What if you can't make good on it? I think I have the right to ask, as an old friend of hers."

"Perhaps you have." Wolfe nodded at him. "I concede it. It's a stratagem, Mr. Degan, directed at myself. By committing myself to Mrs. Molloy, before witnesses, I add to other incentives that of preserving my self-conceit. If the risk of failure is grave for her it is also grave for me."

"You didn't have to make it so damned positive." Degan went to Mrs. Molloy and put a hand on her shoulder. "I hope to God he's right, Selma. It's certainly rough on you. Anything more I can do?"

She said no and thanked him, and I went to the hall to let him out. Back in the office, Saul had moved back to a seat up front, presumably by invitation, and Wolfe was lecturing Mrs. Molloy.

". . . and I'll answer your question, but only on condition that henceforth you confide in no one. You are to tell no one anything you may learn of my surmises or plans.

If I suspected Mr. Degan, as I did and do, I now have better reason to suspect other friends of yours. Do you accept the condition?"

"I'll accept anything that will help," she declared. "All I asked was what he was doing—the man that was killed."

"And I want to tell you because you may be of help, but first I must be assured that you will trust no one. You will repeat nothing and reveal nothing."

"All right. I promise."

Regarding her, he rubbed the end of his nose with a finger tip. It was a dilemma that had confronted him many times over the years. There were very few men whose tongues he had ever been willing to rely on, and no women at all, but she might have facts he needed and he had to risk it. So he did.

"Mr. Keems left here shortly after seven o'clock last evening with specific instructions, to see the three people who were with you at the theater the evening of January third. He was to learn—What's the matter?"

Her chin had jerked up and her lips had parted. "You might have told me that you suspect me too. I suppose you did, when you said you suspect all of my husband's associates."

"Nonsense. His target was not your alibi. He was to learn all the circumstances of the invitation you got to use an extra theater ticket. That was what got you away from your apartment for the evening. Whoever went there to kill your husband certainly knew you were safely out of the way; and not only that, he may have arranged for your absence. That was what Mr. Keems was after. He had the names and addresses of Mr. Irwin and Mr. and Mrs. Arkoff, and he was to report to me at once if he got any hint that the invitation to you was designed. He didn't report, but he must have got a hint, or someone thought he did; and it must have been a betraying hint, since to suppress it someone stole an automobile and killed him with it. That is not palpable, but it's highly probable, and it's my assumption until it's discredited."

"But then—" She shook her head. "I just don't believe— Did he see them? Who did he see?"

"I don't know. As I say, he didn't report. We'll find out.

I want all you can tell me about that invitation. It came from Mrs. Arkoff?"

"Yes. She phoned me."

"When?"

"At half-past seven. I told all about it on the—at the trial."

"I know you did, but I want it first-hand. What did she say?"

"She said that she and Jerry—her husband—had asked Tom and Fanny Irwin to dinner and a show, and she and Jerry were at the restaurant, and Tom had just phoned that Fanny had a headache and couldn't come and he would meet them in the theater lobby, and Rita—that's Mrs. Arkoff—she asked me to come, and I said I would."

"Did you go to the restaurant?"

"No, there wasn't time, and I had to dress. I met them at the theater."

"At what time?"

"Half-past eight."

"They were there?"

"Rita and Jerry were. We waited a few minutes for Tom, and then Rita and I went on in and Jerry waited in the lobby for Tom. Rita told him to leave the ticket at the box office, but he said no, he had told him they'd meet him in the lobby. Rita and I went on in because we didn't want to miss the curtain. It was Julie Harris in *The Lark*."

"How soon did the men join you?"

"It was quite a while. Almost the end of the first act."

"When does the first act end?"

"I don't know. It's rather long."

Wolfe's head moved. "You've seen that play, Archie?"

"Yes, sir. I would say a quarter to ten, maybe twenty to."

"Have you seen it, Saul?"

"Yes, sir. Twenty to ten."

"You know that?"

"Yes, sir. Just my habit of noticing things."

"Don't disparage it. The more you put in a brain, the more it will hold—if you have one. How long would it take to get from One-seventy-one East Fifty-second Street to that theater?"

"After nine o'clock?"

"Yes."

"With luck, if you were in a hurry, eight minutes. That would be a minimum. From that up to fifteen."

Wolfe turned. "Mrs. Molloy, I wonder that you haven't considered the possible significance of this. The anonymous call to the police, saying that a shot had been heard, was at nine-eighteen. The police arrived at nine-twenty-three. Even if he waited to see them arrive, and he probably didn't, he could have reached the theater before the first act ended. Didn't that occur to you?"

She was squinting at him. "If I understand you—you mean didn't it occur to me that Jerry or Tom might have killed Mike?"

"Obviously. Didn't it?"

"No!" She made it a little louder than it had to be, and I hoped Wolfe understood that she was raising her voice not at him, but at herself. It hadn't occurred to her because the minute she had learned, on getting home that January night, that her husband had been found with a bullet in his head, and that P.H., with a gun in his pocket, had tried to force his way out, she thought she knew what had happened, and it had settled in her like a lump of lead. But she wasn't going to tell Wolfe that. She told him instead, "There was no reason for Jerry to kill him. Or Tom. Why? And they had been in the bar across the street. Tom came not long after Rita and I went in, and said he needed a drink, and they went and had one."

"Which one of them told you that?"

"Both of them. They told Rita and me, and we said they must have had more than one."

Wolfe grunted. "Go back a little. Wouldn't it have been the natural thing for Mr. Arkoff to leave the ticket at the box office instead of waiting in the lobby?"

"Not the way it was. Rita didn't ask him to leave it at the box office, she told him to, and he doesn't like to have her tell him to do things. So she does." She came forward in the chair. "Listen, Mr. Wolfe," she said earnestly. "If that man getting killed, if that means what you think it does, I don't care what happens to anybody. I haven't been caring what happened to me, I've just been feeling I might as well be dead, and I'm certainly not going to start worrying about other people, not even my best friends. But I think this is no use. Even if they lied about being in the bar, neither of them had any reason!"

"We'll see about that," he told her. "Someone had reason to fear Johnny Keems enough to kill him." He glanced up at the clock. "Luncheon will be ready in seven minutes. You'll join us? You too, Saul. Afterward you'll stay here to be on hand if Mr. Parker needs you. And Mrs. Molloy, you'll stay too and tell me everything you know about your friends, and you'll invite them to join us here at six o'clock."

"But I can't!" she protested. "How can I? Now?"

"You said you weren't going to worry about them. Yesterday morning Peter Hays, talking with Mr. Goodwin, used the same words you have just used. He said he might as well be dead. I intend that both of you—"

"Oh!" she cried, to me. "You saw him? What did he say?"

"I was only with him a few minutes," I told her. "Except that he might as well be dead, not much. He can tell you himself when we finish this job." I went to Wolfe. "I've got to call Purley. What do I tell him?"

He pinched his nose. He has an idea that pinching his nose makes his sense of smell keener, and a faint aroma of cheese dumplings was coming to us from the kitchen. "Tell him that Mr. Keems was working for me last evening, investigating a confidential matter, but I don't know whom he had seen just prior to his death; and that we'll inform him if and when we get information that might be useful. I want to speak with those people before he does."

As I turned to dial, Fritz entered to announce lunch.

10

Not long ago I got a letter from a woman who had read some of my accounts of Nero Wolfe's activities, asking me why I was down on marriage. She said she was twenty-three years old and was thinking of having a go at it herself. I wrote her that as far as I knew there was absolutely nothing wrong with marriage; the trouble was the way people handled it, and I gave her a couple of examples. The examples I used were Mr. and Mrs. Jerome Arkoff and Mr. and Mrs. Thomas L. Irwin, though I didn't mention their names, and I had got my material from what I saw and heard in the first five minutes after they arrived at Wolfe's place that Thursday at six o'clock.

They all arrived together, and there was a little bustle in the hall, getting their things off and disposed of. That was finished and I was ready to herd them down the hall and into the office when Rita Arkoff touched her husband's elbow, pointed to a chair against the wall, and told him, "Your hat, Jerry. Hang it up."

No wonder he hadn't left the ticket at the box office. Before he could react normally, like making a face at her or telling her to go to hell, I got the hat myself and put it on the rack, and we proceeded to the office, where the Irwins immediately contributed their share. I had the chairs spaced comfortably to give everyone elbow room, but Tom Irwin pushed his close to his wife's, sat, and took her hand in his and held onto it. I am not by any means against holding hands, in wedded bliss or un-wedded, but only if both hands want to, and Fanny Irwin's didn't. She didn't actually try to pull it away, but she sure would have liked to. I hope the examples I gave her will keep my twenty-three-year-old correspondent from developing into an order-giver or a one-way hand-holder, but leave it to her, she'll find some kind of monkey wrench to toss into the machinery, and if she doesn't her husband will.

However, I'm getting ahead of myself. Before six o'clock came, and brought the two couples, there were other happenings. My lunch was interrupted twice. Fred Durkin phoned to say that he had seen the soda jerk who had moved to Jersey, and got nothing, and had worn out his welcome at all places with phone booths within two blocks of 171 East 52nd Street. I told him to come in. Orrie Cather phoned to ask if we had an administrator yet, and I told him also to come in. They arrived before we finished lunch, and, back in the office, Wolfe told them about Johnny Keems.

They agreed with Saul and me that the odds were big that the car that had hit enough of him to kill him had been not careless but careful. They hadn't had much love for him, but they had worked a lot with him. As Fred Durkin said, "Lots of worse guys are still walking around." Orrie Cather said, "Yes, and one of them has got something coming." No one mentioned that until he got it they had better keep an eye out when crossing a street, but they were all thinking it.

They were given errands. Saul was to go to Parker's office to be at hand. Orrie, armed with Selma Molloy's keys, was to go to her apartment and inspect the contents of the three cartons. Fred, supplied by Mrs. Molloy with descriptions of Jerome Arkoff and Tom Irwin, was to go to the Longacre Theatre and the bar across the street and see if he could find someone who could remember as far back as January 3. Fred was getting the scraps.

When they had gone Wolfe tackled Mrs. Molloy again, to get the lowdown on her friends. Using the phone in the kitchen while he was busy with the staff, she had asked them to come to Wolfe's office at six o'clock. I don't know what she had told them, since she couldn't very well say that Wolfe wanted to find out which one of them had killed Mike Molloy, but anyhow they had said they would come. I had suggested that she could tell them that Wolfe was working with Freyer and was trying to find some grounds for an appeal, and probably she did.

Of course Wolfe had her cornered. If there was any chance of springing her P.H. she was all for it, but friends are friends, for people who are entitled to have any, until shown to be otherwise. If you want to take the word of one bewitched, she handled it very nicely. She stuck strictly to facts. For instance, she did not say that Fanny Irwin and Pat Degan were snatching a snuggle; she merely said that Rita Arkoff thought they were.

Jerome Arkoff, thirty-eight, a husky six-footer with a long solemn face, gray-blue eyes, a long nose, and big ears, according to the description she had given Fred Durkin, was a television producer, successful enough to have ulcers. She had met him through Rita, who had been a model when Selma was, and who had married Arkoff about the time Selma had quit modeling and gone to work for Molloy. Arkoff and Molloy had met through their wives' friendship, and there had been nothing special in their relations, either of harmony or of hostility. If there had been anything between them that could possibly have led to murder, Selma knew nothing of it. She conceded it was conceivable that Molloy and Rita had put horns on Arkoff without her ever suspecting it, and Arkoff had removed the blot by blotting out Molloy, but not that he had also framed Peter Hays. Arkoff had liked Peter Hays.

Thomas L. Irwin, forty, was slender, handsome, and dark-skinned, with a skimpy black mustache. He was an executive in a big printing company, in charge of sales. Selma had met him shortly after her marriage, about the same time she had met Patrick Degan. His company did printing for Degan's organization, the Mechanics Alliance Welfare Association, MAWA for short. Fanny Irwin called Degan "Mawa." Irwin and Molloy had got on each other's nerves and had had some fairly hot exchanges, but Selma had never seen any indication of serious enmity.

It was a thin crop. Wolfe poked all around, but the only real dirt he found was Rita Arkoff's suspicion about Fanny Irwin and Pat Degan, and that wasn't very promising. Even if it was true, and even if Irwin had been aware of it or suspected it, he could hardly have expected to relieve his feelings by killing Molloy. Wolfe abandoned it as fruitless and had gone back to the relationships among the men when a phone call came from Saul Panzer, from Parker's office. Some papers were ready for Mrs. Molloy to sign before a notary and would she please come at once. She left, and five minutes later it was four o'clock and Wolfe went up to the plant rooms.

With a couple of hours to go before company was expected, I would have liked to take a trip up to 52nd Street and help Orrie paw through the cartons, but I had been instructed to stay put, and it was just as well. There were phone calls—one from Lon Cohen, one from our client in Omaha, and one from Purley Stebbins, wanting to know if we had got a line on Johnny Keems's movements and contacts Wednesday evening. I told him no and he was skeptical. When the doorbell rang a little after five o'clock I expected to find Purley on the stoop, come to do a little snarling, but it was a stranger—a tall, slim, narrow-shouldered young man, looking very grim. When I opened the door he was going to push right in, but I was wider and heavier than he was. He announced aggressively, "I want to see Archie Goodwin."

"You are."

"I are what?"

"Seeing Archie Goodwin. Who am I seeing?"

"Oh, a wise guy."

We were off to a bad start, but we got it straightened out that he meant that I was a wise guy, not that I was seeing one; and after I had been informed that his name was William Lesser and he was a friend of Delia Brandt I let him in and took him to the office. When I offered him a chair he ignored it.

"You saw Miss Brandt last night," he said, daring me to try to crawl out of it.

"Right," I confessed.

"About a piece about Molloy for some magazine."

"Right."

"I want to know what she told you about her and Molloy."

I swiveled the chair at my desk and sat. "Not standing

up," I told him. "It would take too long. And besides, I'd want—"

"Did she mention me?"

"Not that I remember. I'd want some kind of a reason. You don't look like a city detective. Are you her brother or uncle or lawyer or what?"

He had his fists on his hips. "If I was her brother my name wouldn't be Lesser, would it? I'm a friend of hers. I'm going to marry her."

I raised the brows. "Then you're off on the wrong foot, brother. A happy marriage must be based on mutual trust and understanding, so they say. Don't ask me what she told me about her and Molloy, ask her."

"I don't have to ask her. She told me."

"I see. If that's how it is you'd better sit down. When are you going to be married?"

The chair I had offered was right beside him. He looked at the seat of it as if he suspected tacks, looked back at me, and sat. "Listen," he said, "it's not the way you make it sound. I told her I was coming to see you. It's not that I don't trust her, it's having it come out in a magazine. Haven't I got a right to find out what's going to be printed about my wife and a man she used to work for?"

"You certainly have, but she's not your wife yet. When is the wedding?"

"Right away. We got the license today. Next week."

"Congratulations. You're a lucky man, Mr. Lesser. How long have you known her?"

"About a year. A little over. Now are you going to tell me what I asked?"

"I have no objection." I crossed my legs and leaned back. "This may ease your mind a little, the fact that the magazine wouldn't dream of printing anything Miss Brandt disapproved of, or anything her husband disapproved of. Invasion of privacy. And you've given me an idea. The article would be a lot better with some real love interest. You know what the slant is, the last ten months of a murder victim as seen by his secretary. Well, all the time she is working for him, and letting him take her out to dinner because she feels sorry for him, her heart is already in bond to another. She is deeply in love with a young man she intends to marry. That would make it a masterpiece—the contrast between the tragedy of the man who is going to die but doesn't know it, and the blush and promise of young love. Huh?"

"I guess so. What did she tell you?"

"Don't worry about that." I waved it away. "When it's written you and she can change anything you don't like, or take it out. When were you engaged?"

"Well—it was understood quite a while ago."

"Before the murder?"

"Formally engaged, no. Does that matter?"

"Maybe not. While she's being sorry for Molloy she can either be promised to another or just hoping she soon will be. It would be swell if we could work in some reference, a sort of minor key, to the murderer. We could call him that, since he's been convicted. Only I don't suppose you knew Peter Hays."

"No."

"Did you know about him? Did you know he was in love with Mrs. Molloy?"

"No. I never heard of him until he was arrested."

"It doesn't really matter. I thought perhaps Miss Brandt had mentioned him to you. Of course Molloy told her about him."

"How do you know he did? Did she say so?"

"I don't remember." I considered. "I'd have to look at my notes, and they're not here. Did she tell you about Molloy asking her to go to South America with him?"

"No, she didn't." Lesser was looking aggressive again. "I didn't come to tell you what she told me, I came to ask you what she told you."

"I know you did." I was sympathetic. "But you have my word that nothing will be printed that you don't like, and that's what you were concerned about. I can't tell you about my talk with Miss Brandt because I was working for a client and my report of that talk is his property. But I think—"

"Then you're not going to tell me."

"I'd like to, but I can't. But I think—"

He got up and walked out. From the back he looked even thinner than from the front. I went to the hall to be polite, but he already had his coat off the rack and was reaching for the doorknob. He banged the door shut behind him, and I returned to the office. The wall clock said twenty-five to six. Delia Brandt might have got home from work, or, since she had gone with Lesser to get their marriage license, she might have taken the day off. I got at the phone and dialed the number of her apartment. No answer.

I thought him over. There was one nice thing about him, he had had the makings of a motive, which was more than I could say for anyone else on the list. And he might easily have known enough about Peter Hays to get the idea of framing him for it. But how could he have arranged for Fanny Irwin to have a headache and stay home, and for Rita Arkoff to invite Selma Molloy to use the ticket? Even if that wasn't essential, if he was merely waiting for an opportunity to knock, how did he know it was knocking? How did he know Mrs. Molloy was away from the apartment and would stay away? It was worth looking for answers to those questions, because there was another nice thing about him: a wife cannot be summoned to testify against her husband.

I dialed Delia Brandt's number again, and got her. "I've just heard a piece of news," I told her. "That you're going to be married. I'm calling to wish you luck, and happiness, and everything that goes with it."

"Oh, thank you! Thank you very much. Is Bill there with you?"

"No, he left a few minutes ago. A fine young man. It was a pleasure to meet him. Apparently he was a little worried about the magazine article, but I promised him he would have a chance to veto anything he didn't like. So you knew he was coming to see me?"

"Oh, sure. He said he wanted to, and I thought since he was going to be my husband it was only natural. Did you tell him everything—what did you tell him?"

It didn't look like paradise to me, him wanting to know what she had told me, and her wanting to know what I had told him, and they weren't even married yet. "Nothing much," I assured her. "Really nothing. After the promise I gave him it wasn't necessary. Oh, by the way, now that I have you on the phone, I missed one bet entirely last night. At the end of the article, a sort of a climax, you ought to tell where you were and what you were doing the evening of January third. At the very minute Molloy was murdered, just after nine o'clock, if you remember. Do you?"

"Certainly I do. I was with Bill. We were dining and dancing at the Dixie Bower. We didn't leave until after midnight."

"That's wonderful. That will fit right in with an idea I had and told Bill about, how all the time you were trying to be nice to Molloy because you were sorry for him you were deeply in love with a young man who—"

She cut me off. "Oh, the bell's ringing! It must be Bill."

A little click and she was gone. It didn't matter much, since there was soon an interruption at my end. I had just hung up when the sound came of Wolfe's elevator descending, and he had just entered and was crossing to his desk when the doorbell rang and I had to go to the hall to receive the company. I have already told about that, about Rita Arkoff ordering her mate to hang up his hat, and about Tom Irwin moving his chair next to his wife's and holding her hand. But, looking back, I see that I haven't mentioned Selma Molloy. I could go back and insert her, but I don't care to cover up. I am not responsible for my subconscious, and if it arranged, without my knowing it, to leave Selma out because it didn't want you to know how it felt about her, that's its lookout. I now put her back in. Around five o'clock she had returned from her errand at Parker's office, and, at Wolfe's suggestion, had gone up to the plant rooms to look at the orchids. He had brought her down with him, and she was sitting in the red leather chair, after greeting her friends. Try again, subconscious.

11

The exchange of greetings between Selma and the quartet had seemed a little cramped for old friends, but that might have been expected. After all, she was aiding and abetting a program that might lead to one of them getting charged with murder, and they had been invited by her to the office of a well-known private detective. When they had got seated she sent her eyes to Wolfe and kept them there. Their eyes were more interested in her than in Wolfe. I concentrated on them.

Selma's descriptions of Tom and Jerry had been adequate and accurate. Jerome Arkoff was big and broad, taller than me, and so solemn it must have hurt, but it could have been the ulcers that hurt. Tom Irwin, with his dark skin and thin little clipped mustache, looked more like a saxophone artist than a printing executive, even while holding his wife's hand. His wife, Fanny, was obviously not at her best, with her face giving the impression that she was trying not to give in to a raging headache, but even so she was no eyesore. Under favorable conditions she would have been very decorative. She was a blonde, and a headache is much harder on a bonde than on a brunette; some brunettes are actually improved by a mild one. This brunette, Rita Arkoff, didn't need one. There was a faint touch of snake hips in her walk, a faint suggestion of slant at the corners of her eyes, and a faint hint of a pout in the set of her well-tinted lips. But an order-giver . . .

Wolfe's eyes went from the Arkoffs on his left to the Irwins on the right. "I don't presume," he said, "to thank you for coming, since it was at Mrs. Molloy's request. She has told you what I'm after. Mr. Albert Freyer, counsel for Peter Hays, wishes to establish a basis for a retrial or an appeal, and I'm trying to help him. I assume you are all in sympathy with that?"

They exchanged glances. "Sure we are," Jerome Arkoff declared. "If you can find one. Is there any chance?"

"I think so." Wolfe was easy and relaxed. "Certain aspects have not been thoroughly investigated—not by the police because of the overwhelming evidence against Peter Hays, and not by Mr. Freyer because he lacked funds and facilities. They deserve—"

"Does he have funds now?" Tom Irwin asked. His voice didn't fit his physique. You would have expected a squeak, but it was a deep baritone.

"No. My interest has been engaged, no matter how, and I am indulging it. Those aspects deserve inquiry, and last evening I sent a man to look into one of them—a man named Johnny Keems, who worked for me intermittently. He was to learn if there was any possibility that on the evening the murder was committed, January third, the invitation to Mrs. Molloy to join a theater party had been designed with the purpose of getting her out of the way. Of course it didn't—"

"You sent that man?" Arkoff demanded.

His wife looked reproachfully at her friend. "Selma darling, really! You know perfectly well—"

"If you please!" Wolfe showed her a palm, and his tone sharpened. "Save your resentment for a need; I'm imputing no malignity to any of you. I was about to say, it didn't have to be designed, since the murderer may have merely seized an opportunity; and if it was designed, it didn't have to be one of you who designed it. You might have been quite unaware of it. That was what I sent Mr. Keems to find out, and he was to begin by seeing you, all four of you. First on his list was Mrs. Arkoff, since she had phoned the invitation to Mrs. Molloy." His eyes leveled at Rita. "Did he see you, madam?"

She started to answer, but her husband cut in. "Hold it, Rita." Apparently he could give orders too. He looked at Wolfe. "What's the big idea? If you sent him why don't you ask him? Why drag us down here? Did someone else send him?"

Wolfe nodded. He closed his eyes for a moment, and opened them, and nodded again. "A logical inference, Mr. Arkoff, but wrong. I sent him, but I can't ask him, because he's dead. On Riverside Drive in the Nineties, shortly before midnight last night, an automobile hit him and killed him. It's possible that it was an accident, but I don't think so. I think he was murdered. I think that, working on the assignment I had given him, he had uncovered something that was a mortal threat to someone. Therefore I must see the people he saw and find out what was said. Did he see you, Mrs. Arkoff?"

Her husband stopped her again. "This is different," he told Wolfe, and he looked and sounded different. "If he was murdered. What makes you think it wasn't an accident?"

Wolfe shook his head. "We won't go into that, Mr. Arkoff, and we don't have to because the police also suspect that it wasn't. A sergeant at the Homicide Bureau phoned me today to ask if Mr. Keems was working for me last night, and if so, what his assignment was and whom he had seen. Mr. Goodwin put him off—"

"He phoned again later," I put in.

"Yes? What did you tell him?"

"That we were trying to check and would let him know as soon as we had anything useful."

Wolfe went back to them. "I wanted to talk with you people myself first. I wanted to learn what you had told Mr. Keems, and whether he had uncovered anything that might have threatened one of you or someone else. I'll have—"

Fanny Irwin blurted, "He didn't uncover anything with me!" She had got her hand back from her husband's hold.

"Then that's what I'll learn, madam. I'll have to tell the police what he was to do and whom he was to see; that can't be postponed much longer; but it may make things easier for you if I can also tell them that I have talked with you—depending, of course, on what you tell me. Or would you prefer to save it for the police?"

"My God." Tom Irwin groaned. "This is a nice mess."

"And we can thank you for it," Arkoff told Wolfe. "Sicking your damn snoop on us." His head turned. "And you, Selma. You started it."

"Let Selma alone," Rita ordered him. "She's had a rough time and you can't blame her." She looked at

Wolfe, and she wasn't pouting. "Let's go ahead and get it over with. Yes, your man saw me, at my apartment. He came when I was about ready to leave, to meet my husband for dinner. He said he was investigating the possibility of a new trial for Peter Hays. I thought he was after Selma's alibi and I told him he might as well save his breath because she was with me every minute, but it was the invitation he wanted to ask about. He asked when I first thought of asking Selma, and I said at the restaurant when Tom phoned and told me Fanny couldn't make it. He asked why I asked Selma instead of someone else, and I said because I liked her and enjoyed her company, and also because when Tom phoned I asked him if he wanted to suggest anyone and he suggested Selma. He asked if Tom gave any special reason for having Selma, and I said he didn't have to because I wanted her anyway. He was going to ask more, but I was late and I said that was all I knew anyhow. So that was all—no, he asked when he could see my husband, and I told him we'd be home around ten o'clock and he might see him then."

"Did he?"

"Yes. We got home a little after ten and he was waiting down in the lobby."

Wolfe's eyes moved. "Mr. Arkoff?"

Jerry hesitated, then shrugged. "I talked with him there in the lobby. I didn't take him upstairs because I had some scripts to go over. He asked me the same things he had asked my wife, but I couldn't tell him as much as she had because she had talked with Tom on the phone. I really couldn't tell him anything. He tried to be clever, asking trick questions about how it was decided to invite Mrs. Molloy, and finally I got fed up and told him to go peddle his papers."

"Did he say anything about having seen Mr. or Mrs. Irwin?"

"No. I don't think so. No."

"Then he left?"

"I suppose so. We left him in the lobby when we went to the elevator."

"You and your wife went up to your apartment?"

"Yes."

"What did you do the rest of the evening?"

Arkoff took a breath. "By God," he said, "if anyone had told me an hour ago that I was going to be asked where I was at the time of the murder I would have thought he was crazy."

"No doubt. It does often seem an impertinence. Where were you?"

"I was in my apartment, working with scripts until after midnight. My wife was in another room, and neither of us could have gone out without the other one knowing it. No one else was there."

"That seems conclusive. Certainly either conclusive or collusive." Wolfe's eyes went right. "Mr. Irwin, since Mr. Keems had been told that you had suggested Mrs. Molloy, I presume he sought you. Did he find you?"

From the expression on Tom Irwin's face, he needed a hand to hold. He opened his mouth and closed it again. "I'm not sure I like this," he said. "If I'm going to be questioned about a murder I think I'd rather be questioned by the police."

"Oh, for heaven's sake," his wife protested. "He won't bite you! Do what Rita did, get it over with!" She went to Wolfe. "Do you want me to tell it?"

"If you were present, madam."

"I was. That man—what was his name?"

"John Joseph Keems."

"It was nearly nine o'clock when he came, and we were just going out. We had promised to drop in at a party some friends were giving for somebody, and we would have been gone if my maid hadn't had to fix the lining of my wrap. He said the same thing he told Rita, about the possibility of a new trial for Peter Hays, and he asked my husband about the phone call to the restaurant. Rita has told you about that. Actually—"

"Did your husband's account of it agree with Mrs. Arkoff's?"

"Of course. Why wouldn't it? Actually, though, it was I who suggested asking Selma Molloy. While Tom was at the phone I told him to tell her to ask Selma because I could trust him with her. It was partly a joke, but I'm one

of those jealous wives. Then he wanted to ask some more
questions, I mean that man Keems, but by that time my
wrap was ready and we had told him all we knew. That
was all there was to it."

"Did your husband tell him that you had suggested
asking Mrs. Molloy?"

"Yes, I'm pretty sure— Didn't you, Tom?"

"Yes."

"And you went to the party? How late did you stay?"

"Not late at all. It was a bore, and my husband was tired.
We got home around eleven and went to bed. We sleep in
the same room."

Wolfe started to make a face, realized he was doing it,
and called it off. The idea of sleeping in the same room
with anybody on earth, man or woman, was too much.
"Then," he asked, "you had only that one brief talk with
Mr. Keems? You didn't see him again?"

"No. How could we?"

"Did you see him again, Mr. Irwin?"

"No."

"Can you add anything to your wife's account of your
talk with him?"

"No. That was all there was to it. I might add that our
maid sleeps in, and she was there that night."

"Thank you. That should be helpful. I'll include it in my
report to the police." Wolfe went back to the wife. "One
little point, Mrs. Irwin. If you decided earlier in the day
that you wouldn't be able to go to the theater that evening,
you might have mentioned it to someone, for instance to
some friend on the phone, and you might also have mentioned, partly as a joke, that you would suggest that Mrs.
Molloy be asked in your place. Did anything like that
happen?"

She shook her head. "No, it couldn't have, because I
didn't decide not to go until just before my husband came
home."

"Then your headache was a sudden attack?"

"I don't know what you would call sudden. I was lying
down with it most of the afternoon, and taking emagrin,
and I was hoping it would go away. But I had to give up."

"Do you have frequent headaches?"

Irwin burst out, "What the hell has that got to do with it?"

"Probably nothing," Wolfe conceded. "I'm fishing white water, Mr. Irwin, and am casting at random."

"It seems to me," Arkoff put in, "that you're fishing in dead water. Asking Mrs. Molloy didn't have to be designed at all. If Peter Hays didn't kill Molloy, if someone else did, of course it was somebody who knew him. He could have phoned Molloy and said he wanted to see him alone, and Molloy told him to come to the apartment, they would be alone there because Mrs. Molloy had gone to the theater. Why couldn't it have happened like that?"

"It could," Wolfe agreed. "Quite possible. The invitation to Mrs. Molloy was merely one of the aspects that deserved inquiry, and it might have been quickly eliminated. But not now. Now there is a question that must be answered: who killed Johnny Keems, and why?"

"Some damned fool. Some hit-and-run maniac."

"Possibly, but I don't believe it. I must be satisfied now, and so must the police, and even if you people are innocent of any complicity you can't escape harassment. I'll want to know more than I do now about the evening of January third, about what happened at the theater. I understand— Yes, Archie?"

"Before you leave last night," I said, "I have a question to ask them."

"Go ahead."

I leaned forward to have all their faces as they turned to me. "About Johnny Keems," I said. "Did he ask any of you anything about Bill Lesser?"

They had never heard the name before. You can't always go by the reaction to a sudden unexpected question, since some people are extremely good at handling their faces, but if that name meant anything to one or more of them they were better than good. They all looked blank and wanted to know who Bill Lesser was. Of course Wolfe would also have liked to know who he was but didn't say so. I told him that was all, and he resumed.

"I understand that Mrs. Molloy and Mrs. Arkoff went in to their seats before curtain time, and that Mr. Arkoff and Mr. Irwin joined them about an hour later, saying they had been in a bar across the street. Is that correct, Mr. Arkoff?"

Arkoff didn't care for that at all, and neither did Irwin. Their position was that their movements on the evening of January 3 had no significance unless it was assumed that one or both of them might have killed Molloy and framed Peter Hays, and that was absurd. Wolfe's position was that the police would ask him if he had questioned them about January 3, and if he said he had and they had balked, the police would want to know why.

Rita told her husband to quit arguing and get it over with, and that only made it worse, until she snapped at him, "What's so touchy about it? Weren't you just dosing up?"

He gave her a dirty look and then transferred it to Wolfe. "My wife and I," he said, "met Mrs. Molloy in the theater lobby at half-past eight. The ladies went on in and I waited in the lobby for Irwin. He came a few minutes later and said he wanted a drink, and he also said he didn't care much for plays about Joan of Arc. We went across the street and had a couple of drinks, and by the time we got in to our seats the first act was about over."

Wolfe's head turned. "You corroborate that, Mr. Irwin?"

"I do."

Wolfe turned a hand over. "So simple, gentlemen. Why all the pother? And with a new and quite persuasive detail, that Mr. Irwin doesn't care for plays about Joan of Arc— an inspired hoyden. To show you to what lengths an investigation can be carried, and sometimes has to be, a dozen men could make a tour of Mr. Irwin's friends and acquaintances and ask if they have ever heard him express an attitude toward Joan of Arc and plays about her. I doubt if I'll be driven to that extremity. Have you any questions?"

They hadn't, for him. Rita Arkoff got up and went to Selma, and Fanny Irwin joined them. The men did too, for a moment, and then headed for the hall, and I followed them. They got their coats on and stood and waited, and finally their women came, and I opened the door. As they moved out Rita was telling the men that she had asked Selma to come and eat with them, but she had said she wasn't up to it. "And no wonder," Rita was saying as I swung the door to.

When I re-entered the office Selma didn't look as if she were up to anything whatever, sitting with her shoulders slumped and her head sagging and her eyes closed. Wolfe was speaking, inviting her to stay for not only dinner but also the night. He said he wanted her at hand for consultation if occasion arose, but that wasn't it. She had brought word from Parker that the court formalities might be completed in the morning, and if so we might get to the safe-deposit box by noon. For that Mrs. Molloy would be needed, and Wolfe would never trust a woman to be where she was supposed to be when you wanted her. Therefore he was telling her how pleasant our south room was, directly under his, with a good bed and morning sunshine, but no sale, not even for dinner. She got to her feet, and I went to the hall with her.

"It's hopeless, isn't it," she said, not a question. I patted her shoulder professionally and told her we had barely started.

In the office again, Wolfe demanded, "Who is Bill Lesser?"

I told him, reporting it verbatim, including my phone call to Delia Brandt, and explaining I had hoped to get a glimmer from one or more of the quartet at sound of the name. He wasn't very enthusiastic but admitted it was worth a look and said we would put Fred Durkin on it. I asked if I should phone Purley Stebbins, and he said no, it was too close to dinnertime and he wanted first to think over his talk with Mrs. Molloy's friends.

He heaved a sigh. "Confound it," he complained, "no gleam anywhere, no little fact that stings, no word that trips. I have no appetite!"

I snorted. "That's the least of my worries," I declared.

12

I never did phone Purley because I didn't have to.

Fred Durkin called during dinner and said he had had no better luck at the theater and the bar than at the phone-booth places, and I told him to come in, and he was there by the time we returned to the office with coffee. He had drawn nothing but blanks and I was glad we had a bone for him with a little meat on it. He was to do a take on William Lesser—address, occupation, and the trimmings—and specifically, had he been loose at 11:48 Wednesday night? That last seemed a waste of time and energy, since I had it entered that the Arkoffs and Irwins had never heard of him, but Wolfe wanted a little fact that stung and you never can tell. Just before Fred left Orrie Cather came.

Orrie brought a little package of items he had selected from the cartons in the Molloy apartment, and if they were the cream the milk must have been dishwater. He opened the package on my desk and we went through the treasure together, while Wolfe sat and read a book. There was a desk calendar with an entry on the leaf for January 2, *Call B*, and nothing else; a batch of South American travel folders; half a dozen books of matches from restaurants; a stack of carbon copies of letters, of which the most exciting was one to the Pearson Appliance Corporation telling them what he thought of their electric shaver; and more of the same.

"I don't believe it," I told Orrie. "You must have brought the wrong package."

"Honest to God," he swore. "Talk about drek, I never saw anything to equal it."

"Not even check stubs?"

"Not a stub."

I turned to Wolfe. "Mike Molloy was one of a kind. Meeting sudden death by violence in the prime of his manhood, as you would put it, he left in his office not a single item that would interest a crow, let alone a detective. Not even the phone number of his barber. No gleam anywhere."

"I wouldn't put it that way. Not 'prime of manhood.'"

"Okay. But unless he expected to get killed—"

The doorbell rang. I stepped to the door to the hall, switched on the stoop light, took a look, and turned.

"Cramer. Alone."

"Ah." Wolfe lifted his eyes from the book. "In the front room, Orrie, if you please? Take that stuff with you. When Mr. Cramer has passed through you might as well leave, and report in the morning."

I stood a moment until Orrie had gathered up the treasure and started for the door to the front room, and then went to the hall and opened up. Many a time, seeing the burly breadth and round red face of Inspector Cramer of Homicide there on the stoop, I had left the chain bolt on and spoken with him through the crack, but I now swung the door wide.

"Good evening," I said courteously.

"Hello, Goodwin. Wolfe in?"

That was a form of wit. He knew damn well Wolfe was in, since he was never out. If I had been feeling sociable I would have reciprocated by telling him no, Wolfe had gone skating at Rockefeller Center, but the haul Orrie had brought had been hard on my sense of humor, so I merely admitted him and took his coat. He didn't wait for escort to the office. By the time I got there he was already in the red leather chair and he and Wolfe were glaring at each other. They do that from force of habit. Which way they go from the glare, toward a friendly exchange of information or toward a savage exchange of insults, depends on the circumstances. That time Cramer's opening pass was mild enough. He merely remarked that Goodwin had told Sergeant Stebbins he would call him back and hadn't done so. Wolfe grunted and merely remarked that he didn't suppose Cramer had come in person for information which Mr. Goodwin could have given Mr. Stebbins on the phone.

"But he didn't," Cramer growled.

"He will now," Wolfe growled back. "Do you want him to?"

"No." Cramer got more comfortable. "I'm here now.

There's more to it than Johnny Keems, but I'll take that first. What was he doing for you last night?"

"He was investigating a certain aspect of the murder of Michael M. Molloy on January third."

"The hell he was. I thought a murder investigation was finished when the murderer was tried and convicted."

Wolfe nodded. "It is. But not when an innocent man is tried and convicted."

It looked very much as if they were headed for insults. But before Cramer had one ready Wolfe went on. "You would ask, of course, if I have evidence to establish Peter Hays's innocence. No, I haven't. My reasons for thinking him innocent would not be admissible as evidence, and would have no weight for you. I intend to find the evidence if it exists, and Johnny Keems was looking for it last night."

Cramer's sharp gray eyes, surrounded by crinkles, were leveled at Wolfe's brown ones. He was not amused. On previous occasions, during a murder investigation, he had found Wolfe a thorn in his hide and a pain in his neck, but this was the first time it had ever happened after it had been wrapped up by a jury.

"I am familiar," he said, "with the evidence that convicted Hays. I collected it, or my men did."

"Pfui. It didn't have to be collected. It was there."

"Well, we picked it up. What aspect was Keems working on?"

"The invitation to Mrs. Molloy to go to the theater. On the chance that it was designed, to get her away from the apartment. His instructions were to see Mr. and Mrs. Arkoff and Mr. and Mrs. Irwin, and to report to me if he got any hint of suspicion. He didn't report, which was typical of him, and he paid for his disdain. However, I know that he saw those four, all of them. They were here this afternoon for more than an hour. He saw Mrs. Arkoff at her apartment shortly after eight o'clock, and returned two hours later and saw her and her husband. In between those two visits he saw Mr. and Mrs. Irwin at their apartment. Do you want to know what they say they told him?"

Cramer said he did, and Wolfe obliged. He gave him a full and fair report, including all essentials, unless you

count as an essential his telling them that he wanted to
talk with them before he told the police what Johnny
Keems had been doing—and anyway Cramer could guess
that for himself.

At the end he added a comment. "The inference is patent. Either one or more of them were lying, or Johnny saw
someone besides them, or his death had no connection
with his evening's work. I will accept the last only when I
must, and apparently you will too or you wouldn't be here.
Did the circumstances eliminate fortuity?"

"If you mean could it have been an accident, it's barely
possible. It wasn't on the Drive proper, it was on one of
those narrow side approaches to apartment houses. A man
and woman were in a parked car a hundred feet away, waiting for somone. The car was going slow when it passed
them, going up the lane. They saw Keems step into the lane
from between two parked cars, and they think the driver of
the car blinked his lights, but they're not sure. As the car
approached Keems it slowed nearly to a stop, and then it
took a sudden spurt and swerved straight at Keems, and
that was it. It kept going and had turned a corner before the
man and woman were out of their car. You know we found
the car this morning parked on upper Broadway, and it was
stolen?"

"Yes."

"So it doesn't look like fortuity. I must remember to use
that in a report. You said it could be that one of them was
lying, or more than one. What do you think?"

Wolfe puckered his lips. "It's hard to say. It can't very
well be just one of them, since their alibis are all in pairs—
the two men in the bar the evening of January third, and
for last night man and wife at home together in both cases.
Of course you know their addresses, since you collected the
evidence against Peter Hays."

"They're in the file." Cramer's eyes came to me. "In the
neighborhood, Goodwin?"

"Near enough," I told him. "The Arkoffs in the Eighties
on Central Park West, and the Irwins in the Nineties on
West End Avenue."

"Not that that's important. You understand, Wolfe, as

far as I'm concerned the Hays case is closed. He's guilty as hell. You admit you have no evidence. It's Keems I'm interested in. If it was homicide, homicide is my business. That's what I'm after."

Wolfe's brows went up. "Do you want a suggestion?"

"I can always use a suggestion."

"Drop it. Charge Johnny Keems's death to accident and close the file. I suppose a routine search for the hit-and-run driver must be made, but confine it to that. Otherwise you'll find that the Hays case is open again, and that would be embarrassing. For all I know you may have already been faced with that difficulty and that's why you're here—for instance, through something found in Johnny Keems's pockets. Was there something?"

"No."

Wolfe's eyes were narrowed at him. "I am being completely candid with you, Mr. Cramer."

"So am I. Nothing was found on Keems but the usual items—keys, cigarettes, driving license, handkerchief, a little cash, pen and pencil. After what you tell me I'm surprised he didn't have a memo of those people's names and addresses. Didn't you give him one, Goodwin?"

"No. Johnny didn't believe in memos. He didn't even carry a notebook. He thought his memory was as good as mine, but it wasn't. Now it's no good at all."

He went back to Wolfe. "About your being completely candid, I didn't think I'd go into this, but I will. Tuesday's papers had an ad headed 'To P.H.' and signed by you. Tuesday noon Sergeant Stebbins phoned to ask Goodwin about it, and Goodwin told him to ask Lieutenant Murphy of the Missing Persons Bureau. What he learned from Murphy satisfied him, and me too, that your ad hadn't been directed at Peter Hays but at a man named Paul Herold, and we crossed it off as coincidence. But Wednesday morning, yesterday, Goodwin goes to the City Prison and has a talk with Peter Hays. News of that gets to Murphy, and he sees Hays and asks him if he is Paul Herold, and Hays says no. But here you are saying you think Hays is innocent and up to your neck in it hell for breakfast. If you had Keems investigating one aspect, how many men have you got on other aspects? You don't toss money around just to see it flutter in the breeze. So if you're being so goddam candid, who's your client?"

Wolfe nodded. "That would interest you, naturally. I'm sorry, Mr. Cramer, I can't tell you. You can ask Mr. Albert Freyer, counsel for Peter Hays, and see if you have better luck."

"Nuts. Is Peter Hays Paul Herold?"

"He told Mr. Goodwin he is not. You say he told Lieutenant Murphy he is not. He should know."

"Then why are you on the warpath?"

"Because both my curiosity and cupidity have been aroused, and together they are potent. Believe me, Mr. Cramer, I have been candid to the limit of my discretion. Will you have some beer?"

"No. I'm going. I have to start somebody on these Arkoffs and Irwins."

"Then the Hays case is open again. That is not a gibe, merely a fact. Can you spare me another minute? I would like to know exactly what was found in Johnny Keems's pockets."

"I've told you." Cramer got up. "The usual items."

"Yes, but I'd like a complete list. I would appreciate it, if you'll indulge me."

Cramer eyed him. He could never make up his mind whether Wolfe was really after something or was merely putting on an act. Thinking he might find out, he turned to me. "Get my office, Goodwin."

I swiveled and dialed, and when I had the number Cramer came to my desk and took it. I was supposing he would tell someone to get the list from the file and read it off to me, but no sir. That way I could have faked something, and who would trust Goodwin? He stayed at the phone, and when the list had been dug out and was called off to him he relayed it to me, item by item, and I wrote it down. As follows:

Motor operator's license
Social Security card
Eastern Insurance Co. Identification card
2 tickets to baseball game for May 11th

3 letters in envelopes (personal matters)
Newspaper clipping about fluorine in drinking water
$22.16 in bills and coins
Pack of cigarettes
2 books of matches
4 keys on a ring
1 handkerchief
Ballpoint pen
Pencil
Pocket knife

I started to hand it to Wolfe, but Cramer reached and grabbed it. When he had finished studying it he returned it to me and I passed it to Wolfe, and Cramer asked him, "Well?"

"Thank you very much." Wolfe sounded as if he meant it. "One question: is it possible that something, some small article, was taken from his clothing before this list was made?"

"Possible, yes. Not very likely. The man and woman who saw it from the parked car are respectable and responsible citizens. The man went to where the body was lying, and the woman blew the horn, and an officer came in a couple of minutes. The officer was the first one to touch the body. Why? What's missing?"

"Money. Archie, how much did you give Johnny for expenses?"

"One hundred dollars."

"And presumably he had a little of his own. Of course, Mr. Cramer, I am not ass enough to suggest that you have a thief on your force, but that hundred dollars belonged to me, since Johnny Keems had possession of it as my agent. If by any chance it should turn up—"

"Goddam you, I ought to knock you through that wall," Cramer said through his teeth, and whirled and tramped out.

I waited until I heard the front door slam, then went to the hall and on to the one-way glass panel to see him cross the sidewalk and climb into his car. When I returned to the office Wolfe was sitting with his fingers interlaced at the apex of his central mound, trying not to look smug.

I stood and looked down at him. "I'll be damned," I said. "So you've got your little fact that stings. Next, who did he grease with it?"

He nodded. "Not too difficult, I should think. Apparently you share my assumption that he bribed somebody?"

"No question about it. Johnny wasn't perfect, but he came close to it about money. That hundred bucks was yours, and for him that was that." I sat down. "I'm glad to hear that it won't be difficult to find out who got it. I was afraid it might be."

"I think not—at least not to reach an assumption worth testing. Let us suppose it was you instead of Johnny. Having seen Mrs. Arkoff, you arrive at the Irwins' apartment and find them about ready to leave, being detained by a necessary repair to Mrs. Irwin's garment which is being made by the maid. Mostly they merely confirm what Mrs. Arkoff has already told you, but contribute one new detail: that the suggestion to invite Mrs. Molloy came originally from Mrs. Irwin. That is interesting, even provocative, and you want to pursue it, and try to, but by then the maid has the garment repaired and Mrs. Irwin puts it on, and they leave. You leave with them, of course, going down in the elevator with them, and they go off. There you are. You have seen three of them and have only one more on your list, it's a little after nine o'clock, and there is an hour to pass before you can see Mr. Arkoff. What do you do?"

"Nothing to it. As soon as the Irwins are out of sight I go back upstairs and see the maid."

"Would Johnny?"

"Absolutely."

"Then he did. Worth testing, surely."

"Yeah, it stings, all right. If that maid took your hundred bucks she'll take more." I looked at my wrist. "Ten minutes to eleven. Shall I give her a whirl now?"

"I think not. Mr. and Mrs. Irwin might be there."

"I can phone and find out."

"Do so."

I got the number from the book and dialed it, and after four whirrs a female voice told me hello.

I sent my voice through my nose. "May I speak to Mrs. Irwin, please?"

"This is Mrs. Irwin. Who is this?"

I cradled it, gently, not to be rude, and turned. "Mrs. Irwin answered. I guess it will have to wait until morning. I'll call Mrs. Molloy first and get the maid's name. She probably knows it."

Wolfe nodded. "It will be ticklish, and it must not be botched."

"Right. I'll bring her here and take her to the basement and hold matches to her toes. I have a remark. Your asking Cramer for a list of the contents of Johnny's pockets, that was only par for a genius, but your bumping him off the trail by pretending you wanted your money back—I couldn't have done it better myself. Satisfactory. I hope I'm not flattering you."

"Not likely," he grumbled, and picked up his book.

13

The maid's name was Ella Reyes. I got that from Selma Molloy on the phone at eight o'clock Friday morning, and also that she was around thirty years old, small and neat, the color of coffee with cream, and had been with the Irwins for about a year.

But I didn't get to tackle her. Relieving Fritz of the chore of taking Wolfe's breakfast tray up to his room, where, a mountain of yellow silk pajamas, he stood barefoot in the flood of sunshine near a window, I learned that he had shifted the line-up. Orrie Cather was to call on the man and woman who, sitting in a parked car, had seen the end of Johnny Keems. Their name and address was in the papers, as well as the fact that they agreed that the driver of the hit-and-run car had been a man, and that was about all. They had of course been questioned by old hands at it, but Wolfe wanted Orrie to get it direct.

Saul Panzer was to take the maid, write his own opening,

and ad lib it from there. He was to be equipped with five hundred bucks from the safe, which, added to the C he already had, would make six hundred. A rosy prospect for Ella Reyes, since it would be tax-free. I was to be on call for the ceremony of opening the safe-deposit box, if and when it was scheduled. Wolfe was good enough to supply a reason for giving Saul the maid and me the ceremony. He said that if difficulties arose Mrs. Molloy would be more tractable with me present. Wit.

I was fiddling around the office when Wolfe came down from the plant rooms at eleven o'clock. Saul had arrived at nine and got a thorough briefing and five Cs, and departed, and Orrie had come and gone, to see the eyewitnesses. Parker phoned a little after ten, said he would probably get the court order before noon, and told me to stand by. I asked if I should alert Mrs. Molloy, and he said she wouldn't be needed, so I phoned her that she could relax.

Feeling that the situation called for a really cutting remark to the wit, I concocted a few, but none of them was sharp enough, so when he entered and crossed to his desk I merely said, "Mrs. Molloy isn't coming to the party. You have bewitched her. She admits she wouldn't stay last night because she was afraid to trust herself so close to you. She never wants to go anywhere any more unless you are there."

He grunted and picked up a catalogue that had come in the morning mail, and the phone rang. It was Parker. I was to meet him and Patrick Degan at the Metropolitan Safe Deposit Company at noon.

When I got there, on Madison Avenue in the Forties, five minutes early, I discovered that I hadn't exaggerated when I called it a party, and nobody was late. There were ten of us gathered down in the anteroom of the vaults: Parker; Degan; two officers of the safe deposit company; an attendant of the same; an Assistant District Attorney with a city dick, known to me, apparently as his bodyguard; a fingerprint scientist from the police laboratory, also known to me; a stranger in rimless cheaters whose identity I learned later; and me. Evidently opening a safe-deposit box outside of routine can be quite an affair. I wondered where the mayor was.

After the two MSDC officers had thoroughly studied a

document Parker had handed them we were all escorted through the steel barrier and into a room, not any too big, with three chairs and a narrow table in its center. One of the MSDC officers went out and in a couple of minutes came back, carrying a metal box about twenty-four by eight by six, not normally, but with his fingertips hooked under the bottom edges at front and back. Before an appreciative audience he put it down, tenderly, on the table, and the fingerprint man took the stage, putting his case also on the table and opening it.

I wouldn't say that he stretched it purposely, playing to the gallery, but he sure did an all-out job. He was at it a good half-hour, covering top, sides, ends, and bottom, with dusters, brushes, flippers, magnifying glasses, camera, and print records which came from a brief case carried by the Assistant DA. They should have furnished more chairs.

He handled his climax fine, putting all his paraphernalia back in his case and shutting it before he told us, "I identify six separate prints on the box as the same as those on the records marked Michael M. Molloy. Five other prints are probably the same but I wouldn't certify them. Some other prints may be."

Nobody applauded. Someone sighed, tired of standing up. Parker addressed the stranger with the rimless cheaters. "That meets the provisions of the order, doesn't it?"

"Yes," the stranger conceded, "but I think the expert should certify it in writing."

That started an argument. The expert was allergic to writing. He would maintain his conclusion orally, without reservation, before nine witnesses, but he wouldn't sign a statement until he had made a prolonged study in the laboratory of his photographs and Molloy's recorded prints, and had his findings verified by a colleague. That wasn't very logical, but they couldn't budge him. Finally the stranger said he would stand by his concession that the oral conclusion satisfied the order, and told the MSDC officer to give Parker the box and the key—the duplicate key which had been provided by the MSDC to open the compartment the box had been in. Parker said no, give them to Mr. Degan. But before Degan got them he had to sign a receipt for them.

"All right, open it," the Assistant DA told him.

Degan stood with a hand resting on the box and sent his quick brown eyes around the arc. "Not in public," he said, politely but firmly. "This was Mr. Molloy's box, and I represent his estate by a court order. If you will leave, please? Or if you prefer, I'll take it to another room."

Another argument, a free-for-all. They wanted to see the box opened, but in the end had to give up, when the Assistant DA reluctantly agreed with Parker that Degan's position was legally sound. He left the room, with his bodyguard, and the fingerprint scientist followed them. The two MSDC officers didn't like it at all, but with the law gone they had no choice, so out they went.

Degan looked at the stranger in rimless cheaters and demanded, "Well, sir?"

"I stay," the stranger declared. "I represent the New York State Tax Commission." He was close enough to the table to reach the box by stretching an arm.

"Death and taxes," Parker told Degan. "The laws of nature and the laws of man. You can't budge him. Close the door, Archie."

"Behind you," Degan said. He was looking at Parker. "As you go out."

Parker smiled at him. "Oh, come. Mr. Goodwin and I are not the public. We have a status and a legitimate interest. It was through us that you got that box."

"I know it." Degan kept his hand on it. "But I am now legally in charge of Molloy's estate, temporarily at least, and my only proper obligation is to the estate. You're a lawyer, Mr. Parker, you know that. Be reasonable! What do I actually know about what Nero Wolfe is after or what you're after? Only what you've told me. I don't say that I think you already know about something that's in this box, and that I'm afraid Goodwin will grab it and run, but I do say that it's my responsibility to run no risk of any kind in guarding the estate, and the fact that I got the responsibility through you has nothing to do with it. Isn't that reasonable?" It was an appeal.

"Yes," Parker said, "it's eminently reasonable. I can't challenge it, and I don't. But we're not going to leave. We're not going to grab anything, or even touch anything unless invited, but we're going to see what you find in that box. If you summon help and demand that we be put out I doubt if you'll be obeyed, under the circumstances. If we leave we all leave, and I shall go to Judge Rucker at once and complain that you refuse to open the box in the presence of the widow's counsel. I believe he would enjoin you from opening it at all, pending a hearing."

Degan picked up the box.

"Hold it," I told him. I stepped and closed the door and stepped back. "Mr. Parker has covered most of the ground, but he didn't mention what we'll do if you try moving to another room. That's my department. I'll stand with my back against the door." I moved. "Like this. I'm three inches taller than you and fifteen pounds heavier in spite of your belly, and with the box you'll only have one hand. Of course you can try, and I promise not to hurt you. Much."

He regarded me, not cordially, and breathed.

"This is a farce," Parker declared. He came and joined me with his back against the door. "Now. Now or never. Go ahead and open it. If Goodwin leaps for you I'll trip him. After all, I'm a member of the bar and an officer of the law."

Degan was a stubborn devil. Even then he took another twenty seconds to consider the situation, after which he moved to the far end of the table, facing us at a distance of twelve feet, put the box down, and lifted the lid. The tax man moved with him and was at his elbow. The raised lid obstructed our view, and the inside was not visible, except to him and the New York State Tax Commission. They stared at it a moment, then Degan put a hand in. When he withdrew it, it held a bundle of lettuce three inches thick, fastened with rubber bands. He inspected it all over, put it on the table beside the box, inserted his hand again, and took out another bundle. And others. Eight of them altogether.

He looked at us. "By God," he said, with a little shake in his voice, "I'm glad you fellows stayed. Come and look."

We accepted the invitation. The box was empty. The top bills on five of the bundles were Cs, on two of them fifties, and on the other one a twenty. They were used bills, held tight and compact by the rubber bands. They wouldn't run as healthy as new stuff, around 250 to the inch, but they were not hay.

"Quite a hoard," Parker said. "No wonder you're glad we stayed. If I had been here alone I would have been tempted myself."

Degan nodded, looking dazed. "I'll be damned. We'll have to count it. Will you help me count it?"

We obliged him. I moved the chairs up and we sat, Degan at the table end and Parker and I at either elbow, and started in. The tax man was right behind Degan's shoulder, bending over to breathe down the back of his neck. It took a long while because Degan wanted each bundle counted by all of us, which seemed reasonable, and one of the bundles of fifties had to be gone over six times to reach agreement. When we finished each bundle was topped with a slip of paper with the amount and our initials on it. On another slip Degan listed the amounts and got a total. $327,640.00.

If you don't believe it I'll spell it out. Three hundred and twenty-seven thousand, six hundred and forty berries.

Degan looked at Parker. "You expected this?"

"No. I had no expectations whatever."

He looked at me. "Did you?"

I shook my head. "Same here."

"I wonder. I wonder what Wolfe expected."

"You'd have to ask him."

"I would like to. Is he in his office?"

I looked at my wrist. "He will be for another fifteen minutes. Lunch at one-thirty on Friday."

"We might make it." He returned the bundles to the box, locked it, picked it up, and headed for the door, with the New York State Tax Commission practically stepping on his heels. Parker and I followed, and waited outside while he went with an attendant and the tax man to have the box slid into its niche and locked in, and when he rejoined us we mounted together to the street floor. There the tax man parted from us. Except for interested glances from a couple of guards we drew no attention inside, but the press was on the job. As we emerged to the sidewalk a journalist blocked our path and said the public wanted to know what had been found in Molloy's box, and when we refused to spill it he stayed right with us until we were in the taxi with the door shut.

The midtown traffic kept us from getting to the old brownstone before one-thirty, but since as far as I knew Patrick A. Degan was still a suspect I took him in along with Parker. Herding them into the office, I crossed the hall to the dining room and shut the door. Wolfe, in the big chair with arms, at the far end of the table, had just started operating on an eight-inch ring of ham and sweetbreads mousse.

"You brought visitors," he accused me.

"Yes, sir. Parker and Degan. I know you won't work with the feedbag on, but we found a third of a million dollars in used currency in the safe-deposit box, and Degan wants to ask you if you knew it was there. Shall they wait?"

"Have they eaten?"

"No."

Of course that wouldn't do. The thought of a hungry human, even a hungry murder suspect, even a hungry woman, in his house, is intolerable. So we had luncheon guests. They and I split the mousse that was waiting for me, and while we finished it Fritz manufactured a celery and mushroom omelet. Wolfe tells me there was a man in Marseilles who made a better omelet than Fritz, but I don't believe it. The guests protested that the mousse was all they wanted, but I noticed that the omelet was cleaned up, though I admit Wolfe took a portion just to taste.

Leaving the dining room, I gave Wolfe a sign, and, letting Parker conduct Degan to the office, he and I went to the kitchen, and I reported on the ceremony of opening the box. He listened with a scowl, but not for me. He hates to stand up right after a meal, and he hates to sit down in the kitchen because the stools and chairs aren't fit to sit on—for him.

When I was through he demanded, "How sure are you that the box contained nothing but the money?"

"Dead sure. My eyes were glued to him, and they're good eyes. Not a chance."

"Confound it," he muttered.

"My God," I complained, "you're hard to satisfy. Three hundred and twenty-seven thou—"

"But only that. It's suggestive, of course, but that's all. When a man is involved in a circumstance pressing enough to cause his murder he must leave a relic of it somewhere, and I had hoped it was in that box. Very well. I want to sit down."

He marched to the office, and I followed.

Parker had let Degan have the red leather chair, and Degan had lit a cigar, so Wolfe's nose twitched as he got his bulk adjusted in his chair.

"You gentlemen doubtless have your engagements," he said, "so I apologize for keeping you so long, but I never discuss business at the table. Mr. Goodwin has told me what you found in that box. A substantial nest egg. You have a question for me, Mr. Degan?"

"A couple," Degan said, "but first I must thank you for the lunch. The best omelet I ever ate!"

"I'll tell Mr. Brenner. It will please him. And the question?"

"Well." He blew smoke, straight at his host. "Partly it's just plain curiosity. Were you expecting to find a large sum of money in the box?"

"No. I had no specific expectation. I was hoping to find something that would forward the job I'm on, as I told you yesterday, but I had no idea what it might be."

"Okay." Degan gestured with the cigar. "I'm not a suspicious man, Mr. Wolfe, anyone who knows me will tell you that, but now I've got this responsibility. The thought would have occurred to anybody, finding that fortune in that box, what if you knew it was there or thought it was? And now that it's been found, what if you are figuring that a sizable share of it will be used to pay you for this job you're doing?"

Wolfe grunted. "Surely that's a question for me to ask, not answer. What if I am?"

"Then you are."

"I haven't said so. But what if I am?"

"I don't know. I don't know what to say." Degan took a puff, and this time blew it at Parker. "Frankly, I'm sorry I agreed to this. I did it for a friend who has had a tough break, Selma Molloy, and I wish I hadn't. I'm on a spot. I know she's all for the job you're doing, trying to find grounds for a new trial for Peter Hays, and I am too, personally, so you might think I'd be willing to commit the estate to pay for your services and expenses, but the hell of it is that she says she won't take the estate or any part of it. That didn't matter when there were no visible assets to speak of, but now it does. It will go to someone eventually, relatives always turn up when there's a pile in it, and what will they say if I've paid you some of it? You see my problem." He took a puff.

"I do indeed." Wolfe's lips were slightly twisted—one of his smiles. "But you asked the wrong question. Instead of asking *what* if I am you should have asked *if* I am. The answer is no. I shall not demand, or accept if offered, anything from that trove."

"You won't? You mean that?"

"I do."

"Then why didn't you say so?"

"I have said so." Wolfe's lips straightened. "And now that I have answered your questions, I beg you to reciprocate. You knew Mr. Molloy for some years. Have you any knowledge of the source of that money?"

"No. I was absolutely amazed when I saw it."

"Please bear with me. I don't challenge you, I'm merely trying to stimulate you. You were intimate with him?"

"Intimate? I wouldn't say intimate. He was one of my friends, and I did a little business with him from time to time."

"What kind of business?"

"I bought advice from him now and then." Degan reached to break cigar ash into the tray. "In connection with investments of my organization. He was an expert on certain areas of the real-estate market."

"But you didn't pay him enough to supply an appreciable fraction of that fortune in the box."

"My God, no. On an average, maybe two or three thousand a year."

"Was that the main source of Molloy's income, supplying investment advice regarding real estate?"

"I couldn't say. It may have been, but he did some brokerage and I think he did a little operating on his own. I never heard him say much about his affairs. He had a close mouth."

Wolfe cocked his head. "I appeal to you, Mr. Degan. You had a problem and I relieved you of it. Now I have one. I want to know where that money came from. Surely, in your long association with Mr. Molloy, both business and social, he must have said or done something that would furnish a hint of activities which netted him a third of a million dollars. Surely he did, and if it meant nothing to you at the time, it might now if you recall it. I ask you to make the effort. If, as you said, you wish me success in my efforts on behalf of Mrs. Molloy, I think my request is justified. Don't you agree?"

"Yes, I do." Degan looked at his watch and arose. "I'm late for an appointment. I'll put my mind on it and let you know if I remember anything." He turned, and turned back. "I know a few people who had dealings with Molloy. Do you want me to ask them?"

"Yes indeed. I would appreciate it."

"I suppose you'll ask Mrs. Molloy yourself."

Wolfe said he would, and Degan went. Returning to the office after seeing him out, I stopped at the sill because Parker was on his feet, set to go. He told me not to bother, but I like to be there when the gate of Wolfe's castle opens to the world, so I got his coat from the rack and held it for him.

In the office, Wolfe was having a burst of energy. He had left his chair to get the ashtray Degan had used and was on his way to the door of the bathroom in the corner, to dump it. When he reappeared I asked him, "Nothing from Saul or Fred or Orrie?"

He returned the tray to its place, sat, rang for beer, two short and one long, and roared at me, "No!"

When a hippopotamus is peevish it's a lot of peeve. I should have brought a bundle of Cs for him to play with, and told him so.

How much Wolfe likes to show the orchids to people depends on who it is. Gushers he can stand, and even jostlers. The only ones he can't bear are those who pretend they can tell a P. stuartiana from a P. schilleriana but can't. And there is an ironclad rule that except for Fritz and me, and of course Theodore, who is there all the time, no one goes to the plant rooms for any other purpose than to look at orchids.

Since he refuses to interrupt his two daily turns up there for a trip down to the office, no matter who or what, there have been some predicaments over the years. Once I chased a woman who was part gazelle clear to the top of the second flight before I caught her. The rule hasn't been broken more than half a dozen times altogether, and that afternoon was one of them.

He was in no better mood at four o'clock than an hour earlier. Fred Durkin had come with a report on William Lesser. He was twenty-five years old, lived with his parents on Washington Heights, had been to Korea, was a salesman for a soft-drink distributor, and had never been in jail. No discoverable connection with the Arkoffs or Irwins. No one who had heard him announce that a man named Molloy was going to cart his girl off to South America and he intended to prevent it. No one who knew he had a gun. And more negatives. Wolfe asked Fred if he wanted to try Delia Brandt, disguised as the editor who wanted the magazine article, and Fred said no. As I said before, Fred knows what he can expect of his brains and what he can't. He was told to go and dig some more at Lesser, and went.

Orrie Cather, who came while Fred was there, also drew a blank. The man and woman who had seen the car hit Johnny Keems were no help at all. They were sure the driver had been a man, but whether he was broad or narrow, light or dark, big or little, or with or without a clipped

mustache, they couldn't say. Wolfe phoned Patrick Degan
at his office and got eight names and addresses from him,
friends and associates of Molloy who might furnish some
hint of where the pile had come from, and told Orrie to
make the rounds.

No word from Saul Panzer.

At half-past four I went to answer the doorbell, and
there was the predicament on the stoop. I didn't know it
was the predicament; I thought it was just our client, James
R. Herold of Omaha, coming for a progress report; so I
swung the door wide and welcomed him and took his
things and ushered him to the office and moved a chair so
he would be facing me. I told him on the way that Wolfe
wouldn't be available until six o'clock but I was at his
service. I admit that with the light from the window on
his face I should have guessed he hadn't come merely for
a report. He looked, as he hadn't before, like a man in
trouble. His thin straight mouth was now tight and drawn,
and his eyes were more dead than alive. He spoke. "I'd
rather see Wolfe but I guess you'll do. I want to pay him
to date, the expenses. I'd like to have an itemized account.
Lieutenant Murphy has found my son, and I've seen him.
I won't object if you want to add a small fee to the expenses."

At least I know a predicament when it pushes my nose
in. When a man as pigheaded as Wolfe has ironclad rules
he's stuck with them. If I went upstairs to him and broke
the news there wasn't a chance. He would tell me to tell
Herold that he would like to discuss the matter and would
be down at six o'clock; and it was ten to one, from the
look on Herold's face and the tone of his voice, that he
wouldn't wait. He would say we could mail him a bill and
up and go.

So I stood up. "About the fee," I said, "I wouldn't want
to decide that. That's up to Mr. Wolfe. Come along and
we'll see what he says. This way."

I used the elevator instead of the stairs because the noise
it made would notify Wolfe that something drastic was
happening. Pushing the button to bring it down, entering
with the ex-client, and pushing the button marked R for
roof, my mind wasn't on the predicament at all, it was on

Murphy. If I had had him there I wouldn't have said a word. I wouldn't have bothered with words. As we stopped at the top and the door slid open I told Herold, "I'll lead the way, if you don't mind."

It's hard to believe anyone could go along those aisles without seeing the array of **color at all,** but my mind was on Murphy. I don't know where Herold's was. Wolfe wasn't in the first room, the cool one, nor in the second, the medium, nor in the third, the tropical, and I went on through to the potting room. He was with Theodore at the bench, and turned to glare at us with a pot in one hand and a bunch of sphagnum in the other. With no greeting for the man who, in his ignorance, he thought was still his client, he barked at me, "Why this intrusion?"

"To report," I said. "Mr. Herold just came, and I told him you were engaged and took him to the office, and this is what he said. Quote." I recited Herold's little speech verbatim, and ended, "Unquote."

He had several choices. The rule that nobody came to the roof except to look at orchids had already been broken, by me. He could break the other one by going down to the office with us, or he could tell Herold that he would join him in the office at six o'clock, or he could throw the pot at me. He chose none of them. He turned his back on us, put the pot on the bench, tossed the sphagnum aside, got a trowelful of the charcoal and osmundine mixture from the tub, and dumped it into the pot. He reached for another pot and repeated the operation. And another. When six pots had been prepared he turned around and spoke.

"You have a record of the expenses, Archie."

"Yes, sir."

"Invoice them, including the commitments for today, and add the fee. The fee is fifty thousand dollars."

He turned to the bench and picked up a pot. I said, "Yes, sir," turned to go, and told Herold, "Okay, he's the boss."

"He's not my boss." He was staring at Wolfe's back, which is an eyeful. "You don't mean that. That's ridiculous!'" No reaction. He took a step and raised his voice. "You haven't earned any fee at all! Lieutenant Murphy phoned me last night, and I took a plane, and he arranged for me to see my son. Do you even know where he is? If you do, why didn't you tell me?"

Wolfe turned and said quietly, "Yes, I know where he is. I suspect you, Mr. Herold."

"You suspect me? Of what?"

"Of chicanery. Mr. Murphy has his own credit and glory to consider, and so couldn't be expected to toot my horn, but I do not believe he made no mention of the part I've played. He's not an utter fool. I think you came here aware that I have earned a fee and conceived a shoddy stratagem to minimize it. The fee is fifty thousand dollars."

"I won't pay it!"

"Yes, you will." Wolfe made a face. "I don't run from contention, sir, but this sort of squabble is extremely distasteful. I'll tell you briefly how it will go. I'll render my bill, you'll refuse to pay it, and I'll sue you. By the time the action goes to trial I shall be armed with evidence that I not only found your son, which is what you hired me to do, but that I also freed him from a charge of murder by proving his innocence. Actually I doubt if you'll let it go to trial. You'll settle."

Herold looked around, saw a big comfortable chair, moved to it, and sat. Presumably he had had a tough day.

"That's my chair," Wolfe snapped. He can snap. "There are stools."

Three sound reasons: one, he didn't like Mr. Herold; two, he wanted to squash him; and three, if it went on he might want the chair himself. If Herold got to his feet and stayed on them he was still a contender; if he stayed in the chair he was cornered; if he took to a stool he was licked. He went to a stool and got on it. He spoke, not squabbling.

"Did you say you can prove his innocence?"

"No. Not now. But I expect to." Wolfe propped the back of his lap against the bench. "Mr. Goodwin saw him and talked with him Wednesday morning, day before yesterday, and established that he is your son. He didn't want you to be notified. That's an understatement. Did you speak with him today?"

"I saw him. He wouldn't speak to me. He denied me. His mother is coming."

That was some improvement. Before it had been only "my wife." Now it was "his mother." One big unhappy family.

He went on. "I didn't want her to, but she's coming. I don't know whether he'll speak to her or not. He hasn't just been arrested, he's been convicted, and the District Attorney says there can't be any question about it. What makes you think he's innocent?"

"I don't think it, I know it. One of my men has been killed—and I haven't earned a fee? Pfui. You'll know about it when the time comes."

"I want to know about it now."

"My dear sir." Wolfe was scornful. "You have fired me. We are adversaries in a lawsuit, or soon will be. Mr. Goodwin will conduct you downstairs." He turned, picked up a pot, and got a trowelful of the charcoal-osmundine mixture. That, by the way, was fake. You don't put that mixture in a pot until you have covered the bottom with crock.

From his perch on the stool Herold had him more in profile than full-face. He watched for four pots and then spoke. "I haven't fired you. I didn't know what the situation was. I don't now, and I want to."

Wolfe asked, not turning, "You want me to go on?"

"Yes. His mother is coming."

"Very well. Archie, take Mr. Herold to the office and tell him about it. Omit our inference from the contents of Johnny's pockets. We can't risk Mr. Cramer's meddling in that for the present."

I asked, "Give him everything else?"

"You might as well."

Getting down off the stool, Herold tripped on his own toe and nearly fell. To give him footwork practice I took him back down by way of the stairs.

He wasn't much impressed by my outline of the situation, but he had probably had all the impressions he had room for in one day. The guy was in shock. However, when he left we were still hired. He gave me the name of his hotel, and I said we would report any developments. At the door I told him it wouldn't be a good idea for his wife to come to see Wolfe, because when Wolfe was deep in a case he was apt to forget his manners. I didn't add that he was apt to forget his manners when he wasn't deep in a case.

Alone again, I had a notion to try a few phone calls. In discussing an assignment for Orrie we had considered my tail—the party in a tan raglan and a brown snap-brim who had started to stalk me Tuesday afternoon when I left the house to go to the courtroom for a look at Peter Hays. Since there had been no sign of him since, the assumption was that somebody's curiosity had been aroused by the newspaper ad and he had lost interest after the jury had settled Hays's hash. We had decided it would be useless to put Orrie on it, since there was nowhere to start, but it wouldn't do any harm for me to phone a few of the agencies I was acquainted with and chat a little. The chance was slim that one of them had been hired to put a man on me, and slimmer still that they would spill it to me, but things do sometimes slip out in a friendly conversation, and I might as well be trying it as merely sitting on my fanny. I considered it, and decided to hit Del Bascom first, and was just starting to dial when two interruptions came at once. Wolfe came down from the plant rooms and Saul Panzer arrived.

Saul's face will never tell you a damn thing when he's playing poker with you, or playing anything else that calls for cover, but he's not so careful with it when he doesn't have to be, and at sight of it as I let him in I knew he had something hot.

Wolfe knew it too, and he was on edge. As Saul was turning a chair around he demanded, "Well?"

Saul sat. "From the beginning?"

"Yes."

"I phoned the apartment at nine-thirty-two and a woman answered and I asked to speak to Ella Reyes. She asked who I was and I said a Social Security investigator. She asked what I wanted with Ella Reyes and I said there was apparently a mix-up in names and I wanted to check. She said she wasn't there, and she wasn't sure when she would be, and I thanked her. So already it had a twist. A maid who sleeps in wasn't there and it wasn't known when she would be. I went to the apartment house and identified myself to the doorman."

You should hear Saul identifying himself. What he meant was that after three minutes with the doorman they were on such good terms that he was allowed to take the elevator without a phone call to announce him. It's no good trying to imitate him; I've tried it.

"I went up to Apartment Twelve-B, and Mrs. Irwin came to the door. I told her I had another errand in the neighborhood and dropped in to see Ella Reyes. She said she wasn't there and still didn't know when she would be. I pressed a little, but of course I couldn't over-do it. I said the mix-up had to do with addresses, and maybe she could straighten it out, and asked if her Ella Reyes had another address, perhaps her family's address, at Two-nineteen East One-hundred-and-twelfth Street. She said not that she knew of, that her Ella Reyes' family lived on East One-hundred-and-thirty-seventh Street. I asked if she could give me the number, and she went to another room and came back and said it was Three-oh-six East One-hundred-and-thirty-seventh Street."

Saul looked at me. "Do you want to note that, Archie?" I did so and he resumed. "I went down and asked the doorman if he had noticed Mrs. Irwin's maid going out this morning, and he said no, and he hadn't noticed her coming in either. He said Thursday was her night out and she always came in at eight o'clock Friday morning and he hadn't seen her. He asked the elevator man, and he hadn't seen her either. So I went to Three-oh-six East One-hundred-and-thirty-seventh Street. It's a dump, a cold-water walk-up. I saw Ella Reyes' mother. I was as careful as possible, but it's hard to be careful enough with those people. Anyway, I got it that Ella always came home Thursday nights and she hadn't showed up. Mrs. Reyes had been wanting to go to a phone and call Mrs. Irwin, but she was afraid Ella might be doing something she wouldn't want her employer to know about. She didn't say that, but that's what it was.

"I spent the rest of the day floundering around. Back at the Irwins' address the doorman told me that Ella Reyes

had left as usual at six o'clock yesterday, alone. Mrs. Reyes
had given me the names of a couple of Ella's friends, and
I saw them, and they gave me more names. Nobody had
seen her or heard from her. I phoned Mrs. Irwin twice during the afternoon, and I phoned headquarters once an
hour to ask about accidents, of course not mentioning Ella
Reyes. My last call to headquarters, at five o'clock, I was
told that the body of a woman had been found behind
a pile of lumber on the Harlem River bank near One-
hundred-and-fortieth Street, with nothing on it to identify it. The body was on its way to the morgue. I went
there, but the body hadn't arrived yet. When it came I
looked at it, and it fits Mrs. Molloy's description of Ella
Reyes—around thirty, small and neat, coffee with cream.
Only the head wasn't neat. The back of the skull was
smashed. I just came from there."

I stood up, realized that that didn't help matters any,
and sat down. Wolfe took a long deep breath through
his nose, and let it out through his mouth.

"I needn't ask," he said, "if you communicated your
surmise."

"No, sir. Of course not. A surmise isn't enough."

"No. What time does the morgue close?"

That's one way I know he's a genius. Only a genius
would dare to ask such a question after functioning as a
private detective for more than twenty years right there
in Manhattan, and specializing in murder. The hell of it
was, he really didn't know.

"It doesn't close," Saul said.

"Then we can proceed. Archie. Call Mrs. Molloy and
ask her to meet you there."

"Nothing doing," I said firmly. "There are very few
women I would ask to meet me at the morgue, and Mrs.
Molloy is not one of them. Anyway, her phone may be
tapped. This sonofabitch probably taps lines in between
murders to pass the time. I'll go and get her."

"Then go."

I went.

15

I sat on a chair facing her. I had accepted the offer of a chair because on the way uptown in the taxi I had made a decision which would prolong my stay a little. She was wearing a light weight woolen dress, lemon-colored, which could have been Dacron or something, but I prefer wool.

"When I first saw you," I told her, "fifty hours ago, I might have bet you one to twenty that Peter Hays would get clear. Now it's the other way around. I'll bet you twenty to one."

She squinted at me, giving the corners of her eyes the little upturn, and her mouth worked. "You're just bucking me up," she said.

"No, I'm not, but I admit it's a lead. We need your help. You remember I phoned you this morning to get the name of Mrs. Irwin's maid and a description of her. A body of a woman with a battered skull was found today behind a lumber pile on One-hundred-and-fortieth Street, and it is now in the morgue. We think it's Ella Reyes but we're not sure, and we need to know. I'm going to take you down there to look. It's your turn."

She sat and regarded me without blinking. I sat and waited. Finally she blinked.

"All right," she said, "I'll go. Now?"

No shivers or shudders, no squeals or screams, no string of questions. I admit the circumstances were very favorable, since one thing was so heavy on her mind that there was no room for anything else.

"Now it is," I told her. "But you'll pack a bag for a night or two and we'll take it along. You'll stay at Wolfe's house until this thing is over."

She shook her head. "I won't do that. I told you yesterday. I have to be alone. I can't be with people and eat with people."

"You don't have to. You can have your meals in your

room, and it's a nice room. I'm not asking you, lady, I'm telling you. Fifty hours ago I had to swallow hard to keep from having personal feelings about you, and I don't want to do it again, as I would have to if you were found with your skull battered. I'm perfectly willing to help get your guy out to you alive, but not to your corpse. This specimen has killed Molloy, and Johnny Keems, and now Ella Reyes. I don't know his reason for killing her, but he might have as good a one for killing you, or think he had, and he's not going to. Go pack a bag, and step on it. We're in a hurry."

I'll be damned if she didn't start to reach out a hand to me and then jerk it back. The instinct of a woman never to pass up an advantage probably goes back to when we had tails. But she jerked it back.

She stood up. "I think this is foolish," she said, "but I don't want to die now." She left me.

Another improvement. It hadn't been long since she had said she might as well be dead. She reappeared shortly with a hat and jacket on and carrying a brown leather suitcase. I took the case, and we were off.

To save time I intended to explain the program en route in the taxi, but I didn't get to. After I had told the hackie, "City Mortuary, Four hundred East Twenty-ninth," and he had given us a second look, and we had started to roll, she said she wanted to ask me a question and I told her to shoot.

She moved closer to me to get her mouth six inches from my ear, and asked, "Why did Peter try to get away with the gun in his pocket?"

"You really don't know," I said.

"No, I—How could I know?"

"You might have figured it out. He thought your fingerprints were on the gun and he wanted to ditch it."

She stared. Her face was so close I couldn't see it. "But how could—No! He couldn't think that! He couldn't!"

"If you want to keep this private, tone it down. Why couldn't he? You could. Sauce for the goose and sauce for the gander. You are now inclined to change your mind, but you have been worked on. He hasn't been in touch as you have, so I suppose he still thinks it. Why shouldn't he?"

"Peter thinks I killed Mike?"

"Of course. Since he knows he didn't. Goose is right."

She gripped my arm with both hands. "Mr. Goodwin, I want to see him. I've got to see him *now!*"

"You will, but not where we're going and not now. And for God's sake don't crumple on me at this point. Steady the nerves and stiffen the spine. You've got a job to do. I should have stalled and saved it for later, but you asked me."

So when the cab stopped at the curb in front of the morgue I hadn't briefed her, and, not caring to share it with the hackie, I told him to wait, with the suitcase as collateral, helped her out, and walked her down to the corner and back. Uncertain of the condition of her wits after the jolt I had given her, I made darned sure she had the idea before going inside.

Since I was known there, I had considered sending her in alone, but decided not to risk it. In the outer room I told the sergeant at the desk, whose name was Donovan, that my companion wanted to view the body of the woman which had been found behind a lumber pile. He put an eye on Mrs. Molloy.

"What's her name?"

"Skip it. She's a citizen and pays her taxes."

He shook his head. "It's a rule, Goodwin, and you know it. Give me a name."

"Mrs. Alice Bolt, Churchill Hotel."

"Okay. Who does she think it is?"

But that, as I knew, was not a rule, so I didn't oblige. After a brief wait an attendant who was new to me took us through the gate and along the corridor to the same room where Wolfe had once placed two old dinars on the eyes of Marko Vukcic's corpse. Another corpse was now stretched out on the long table under the strong light, with its lower two-thirds covered with a sheet. At the head an assistant medical examiner whom I had met before was busy with tools. As we approached he told me hello, suspended operations, and backed up a step. Selma had her fingers around my arm, not for support, but as part of the program. The head of the object was on its side, and Selma stooped for a good view at a distance of twenty inches. In four seconds she straightened up and squeezed my arm, two little squeezes.

"No," she said.

It wasn't in the script that she was to hang onto my arm during our exit, but she did, out to the corridor and all the way to the gate and on through. In the outer corridor I broke contact to cross to the desk and tell Donovan that Mrs. Bolt had made no identification, and he said that was too bad.

On the sidewalk I stopped her before we got in earshot of the hackie and asked, "How sure are you?"

"I'm positive," she said. "It's her."

Crossing town on 34th Street can be a crawl, but not at that time of day. Selma leaned back with her eyes closed all the way. She had had three severe bumps within the hour: learning that her P.H. thought she had killed her husband, taking it that he hadn't, and viewing a corpse. She could use a recess.

So when we arrived at the old brownstone I took her up the stoop and in, told her to follow me, and, with the suitcase, mounted one flight to the South Room. It was too late for sunshine, but it's a nice room even without it. I turned on the lights, put the suitcase on the rack, and went to the bathroom to check towels and soap and glasses. She sank into a chair. I told her about the two phones, house and outside, said Fritz would be up with a tray, and left her.

Wolfe was in the dining room, staving off starvation, with Saul Panzer doing likewise, and Fritz was standing there.

"We have a house guest," I told them. "Mrs. Molloy. With luggage. I showed her how to bolt the door. She doesn't feel like eating with people, so I suppose she'll have to get a tray."

They discussed it. The dinner dish was braised pork filets with spiced wine, and they hoped she would like it. If she didn't, what? It was eight o'clock, and I was hungry, so I left it to them and went to the kitchen and dished up a plate for myself. By the time I returned the tray problem had been solved, and I took my place, picked up my knife and fork, and cut into a filet.

I spoke. "I was just thinking, as I dished this pork, about the best diet for a ballplayer. I suppose it depends on the player. Take a guy like Campanella, who probably has to regulate his intake—"

"Confound you, Archie."

"What?" I raised my brows. "No business talk at the table is your rule, not mine. But to change the subject, just for conversation, the study of the human face under stress is absolutely fascinating. Take, for instance, a woman's face I was studying just half an hour ago. She was looking at a corpse and recognizing it as having belonged to a person she knew, but she didn't want two bystanders to know that she recognized it. She wanted to keep her face deadpan, but under the circumstances it was difficult."

"That must have been interesting," Saul said. "You say she recognized it?"

"Oh, sure, no question about it. But you gentlemen continue the conversation. I'm hungry." I forked a bite of filet to my mouth.

It was a tough day for rules. Still another one got a dent when, the dessert having been disposed of, we went to the office for coffee, but that happened fairly often.

I reported, in detail as usual, but not in full. Certain passages of my talk with Mrs. Molloy were not material, and neither was the fact that she had started to put out a hand to me and jerked it back. We discussed the situation and the outlook. The obvious point of attack was Mr. and Mrs. Thomas L. Irwin, but the question was how to attack. If they denied any knowledge of the reason for their maid's absence, and if, told that she had been murdered, they denied knowledge of that too, what then? Saul and I did most of the talking. Wolfe sat and listened, or maybe he didn't listen.

But the only point in keeping the identity of the corpse to ourselves was to have first call on the Irwins and Arkoffs, and if we weren't going to call we might as well let the cops take over. Of course they were already giving the lumber pile and surroundings the full routine, and putting them on to the Irwins and Arkoffs wouldn't help that any, but someone who knew what the medical examiner gave as the time of death should at least ask them where they were between this hour and that hour Thursday night. That was only common politeness.

When Fritz came to bring beer and reported that Mrs. Molloy had said she liked the pork very much but had eaten only one small piece of it, Wolfe told me to go and see if she was comfortable. When I went up I found that she hadn't bolted the door. I knocked and got a call to enter, and did so. She was on her feet, apparently doing nothing. I told her that if she didn't care for the books on the shelf there were a lot more downstairs, and asked if she wanted some magazines or anything else. While I was speaking the doorbell rang downstairs, but with Saul there I skipped it. She said she didn't want anything; she was going to bed and try to sleep.

"I hope you know," she added, "that I realize how wonderful you are. And how much I appreciate all you're doing. And I hope you won't think I'm just a silly goose when I ask if I can see Peter tomorrow. I want to."

"I suppose you could," I said. "Freyer might manage it. But you shouldn't."

"Why not?"

"Because you're the widow of the man he's still convicted of murdering. Because there would be a steel lattice between you with guards present. Because he would hate it. He still thinks you killed Molloy, and that would be a hell of a place to try to talk him out of it. Go to bed and sleep on it."

She was looking at me. She certainly could look straight at you. "All right," she said. She extended a hand. "Good night."

I took the hand in a professional clasp, left the room, pulling the door shut as I went, and went back down to the office to find Inspector Cramer sitting in the red leather chair and Purley Stebbins on one of the yellow ones, beside Saul Panzer.

16

As I circled around Saul and Purley to get to my desk Cramer was speaking.

". . . and I'm fed up! At one o'clock yesterday afternoon Stebbins phoned and told Goodwin about Johnny Keems and asked him if Keems was working for you, and Goodwin said he would have to ask you and would call back. He didn't. At four-thirty Stebbins phoned again, and Goodwin stalled him again. At nine-thirty last evening I came to see you, and you know what you told me. Among other things—"

"Please, Mr. Cramer." Wolfe might have been gently but firmly stopping a talky brat. "You don't need to recapitulate. I know what has happened and what was said."

"Yeah, I don't doubt it. All right, I'll move to today. At five-forty-two this afternoon Saul Panzer is waiting at the morgue to view a body when it arrives, and he views it, and beats it. At seven-twenty Goodwin shows up at the morgue to view the same body, and has a woman with him, and he says they can't identify it and goes off with the woman. He gives her name as Mrs. Alice Bolt— Mrs. Ben Bolt, I suppose—and her address as the Churchill Hotel. There is no Mrs. Bolt registered at the Churchill. So you're up to your goddam tricks again. You not only held out on us about Keems for eight hours yesterday, you held out on me last night, and I'm fed up. Facts connected with a homicide in my jurisdiction belong to me, and I want them."

Wolfe shook his head. "I didn't hold out on you last night, Mr. Cramer."

"Like hell you didn't!"

"No, sir. I was at pains to give you all the facts I had, except one, perhaps—that despite Peter Hays's denial we had concluded he is Paul Herold. But you took care of that, characteristically. Knowing, as you did, that James

R. Herold was my client, you notified him that you thought you had found his son and asked him to come and verify it, omitting the courtesy of even telling me you had done so, let alone consulting me in advance. Considering how you handle facts I give you, it's a wonder I ever give you any at all."

"Nuts. I didn't notify James R. Herold. Lieutenant Murphy did."

"After you had told him of your talk with me." Wolfe flipped a hand to push it aside. "However, as I say, I gave you all the facts I had relevant to your concern. I reported what had been told me by Mr. and Mrs. Arkoff and Mr. and Mrs. Irwin. And I made a point of calling to your attention a most significant fact—more than significant, provocative—the contents of Johnny Keems pockets. You knew, because I told you, these things: that Keems left here at seven-thirty Wednesday evening to see the Arkoffs and Irwins, with a hundred dollars in his pocket for expenses; that during his questioning of the Irwins their maid had been present, and the questioning had been cut short by the Irwins' departure; and that only twenty-two dollars and sixteen cents had been found on his body. I gave you the facts, as of course I should, but it was not incumbent on me to give you my inference."

"What inference?"

"That Keems had spent the hundred dollars in pursuance of his mission, that the most likely form of expenditure had been a bribe, and that a probable recipient of the bribe was the Irwins' maid. Mr. Goodwin got the maid's name, and a description of her, from Mrs. Molloy, and Mr. Panzer went to see her and couldn't find her. He spent the day at it and was finally successful. He found her at the morgue, though the identification was only tentative until Mrs. Molloy verified it."

"That's not what Goodwin told Donovan. He said she couldn't make an identification."

"Certainly. She was in no condition to be pestered. Your colleagues would have kept at her all night. I might as well save you the trouble of a foray on her apartment.

She is in this house, upstairs asleep, and is not to be disturbed."

"But she identified that body?"

"Yes. Positively. As Miss Ella Reyes, the Irwins' maid."

Cramer looked at Stebbins, and Stebbins returned it. Cramer took a cigar from his pocket, rolled it between his palms, and stuck it in his mouth, setting his teeth in it. I have never seen him light one. He looked at Stebbins again, but the sergeant had his eyes at Wolfe.

"I realize," Wolfe said, "that this is a blow for you and you'll have to absorb it. It is now next to certain that an innocent man stands convicted of murder on evidence picked up by your staff, and that's not a pleasant dose—"

"It's far from certain."

"Oh, come, Mr. Cramer. You're not an ass, so don't talk like one. Keems was working on the Molloy murder, and he was killed. He made a contact with Ella Reyes, and she was killed—and by the way, what money was found on her, if any?"

Cramer took a moment to answer, because he would have preferred not to. But the newspaper boys probably already had it. Even so, he didn't answer, he asked, and not Wolfe, but me.

"Goodwin, the hundred you gave Keems. What was it?"

"Five used tens and ten used fives. Some people don't like new ones."

His sharp gray eyes moved. "Was that it, Purley?"

"Yes, sir. No purse or handbag was found. There was a wad in her stocking, ten fives and five tens."

Wolfe grunted. "They belong to me. And speaking of money, here's another point. I suppose you know that I learned that Molloy had rented a safe-deposit box under an alias, and a man named Patrick A. Degan was appointed administrator of the estate, and in that capacity was given access to the box. The safe-deposit company had to have a key made. When Mr. Degan opened the box, with Mr. Goodwin and Mr. Parker present, it was found to contain three hundred and twenty-seven thousand, six hundred and forty dollars in currency. But—"

"I didn't know that."

"Mr. Degan will doubtless confirm it for you. But the point is, where is Molloy's key to that box? Almost certainly he carried it on his person. Was it found on his corpse?"

"Not that I remember." Cramer looked at Stebbins. "Purley?"

Stebbins shook his head.

"And Peter Hays, caught, as you thought, red-handed. Did he have it?"

"I don't think so. Purley?"

"No, sir. He had keys, but none for a safe-deposit box."

Wolfe snorted. "Then consider the high degree of probability that Molloy was carrying the key and the certainty that it was not found on him or on Peter Hays. Where was it? Who took it? Is it still far from certain, Mr. Cramer?"

Cramer put the cigar in his mouth, chewed on it, and took it out again. "I don't know," he rasped, "and neither do you, but you sure have stirred up one hell of a mess. I'm surprised I didn't find those people here—the Arkoffs and Irwins. That must be why you were saving the identification, to have a crack at them before I did. I'm surprised I didn't find you staging one of your goddam inquests. Are they on the way?"

"No. Mr. Goodwin and Mr. Panzer and I were discussing the situation. I don't stage an inquest, as you call it, until I am properly equipped. Obviously the question is, where did Keems go and whom did he see after he talked with the maid? The easiest assumption is that he stayed at the Irwins' apartment until they came home, but there is nothing to support it, and that sort of inquiry is not my métier. It is too laborious and too inconclusive, as you well know. Of course your men will now question the doorman and elevator man, but even if they say that Keems went up again shortly after he left Wednesday night with the Irwins, and didn't come down until after the Irwins returned, what if the Irwins simply deny that he was there when they came home—deny that they ever saw or heard of him again after they left?"

Wolfe gestured. "However, I am not deprecating such

inquiry—checking of alibis and all the long and intricate routine—only I have neither the men nor the temper for it, and you have. For it you need no suggestions from me. If, for example, there is discoverable evidence that Keems returned to the Arkoffs' apartment after talking with Ella Reyes, you'll discover it, and you're welcome to. I'm quite willing for you to finish the job. Since you don't want two unsolved homicides on your record you'll use all your skills and resources to solve them, and when you do you will inevitably clear Peter Hays. I've done my share."

"Yeah. By getting two people murdered."

"Nonsense. That's childish, Mr. Cramer, and you know it."

Stebbins made a noise, and Cramer asked him, "You got a question, Purley?"

"Not exactly a question," Purley rumbled. He was always a little hoarser than normal in Wolfe's presence, from the strain of controlling his impulses. Or rather, one impulse, the one to find out how many clips it would take to make Wolfe incapable of speech. He continued. "Only I don't believe it, that Wolfe's laying off. I never saw him lay off yet. He's got something he's holding onto, and when we've got the edges trimmed by doing all the work that he's too good for he'll spring it. Why has he got that Molloy woman here? You remember the time we got a warrant and searched the whole damn house, and up in the plant rooms he had a woman stretched out in a box covered with moss or something and he was spraying it with water, which we found out later. I can go up and bring her down, or we can both go up. Goodwin won't try stopping an officer of the law, and if he—"

He stopped and was on his feet, but I had already buzzed the South Room on the house phone and in a second was speaking.

"Archie Goodwin, Mrs. Molley. Bolt your door, quick. Step on it. I'll hold on."

"It's already bolted. What—"

"Fine. Sorry to bother you, but a character named Stebbins, a sort of a cop, is having trouble with his brain, and I thought he might go up and try to annoy you. Forget

it, but don't unbolt the door for anybody but me until
further notice."

I hung up and swiveled. "Sit down, Sergeant. Would
you like a glass of water?"

The cord at the side of his big neck was tight. "We're
in the house," he told Cramer, hoarser than ever, "and
they're obstructing justice. She recognized a corpse and
denied it. She's a fugitive. To hell with the bolt."

He knew better, but he was upset. Cramer ignored him
and demanded of Wolfe, "What does Mrs. Molloy know
that you don't want me to know?"

"Nothing whatever, to my knowledge." Wolfe was
unruffled. "Nor do I. She is my guest. It would be vain
to submit her to your importunity even if you requested it
civilly, and Mr. Stebbins should by now know the folly
of trying to bully me. If you wish the identification con-
firmed, why not Mr. or Mrs. Irwin or a member of Ella
Reyes' family? The address is—Saul?"

"Three-oh-six East One-hundred-and-thirty-seventh
Street."

Purley got out his notebook and wrote. Cramer threw
the chewed cigar at my wastebasket, missing as usual,
and stood up. "This may be the time," he said darkly, "or
it may not. The time will come." He marched out, and
Purley followed. I left it to Saul to see them out, thinking that as Purley passed by at the door he might accidentally get his fist in my eye and I might accidentally get my
toe on his rump, and that would only complicate matters.

When Saul came back in, Wolfe was leaning back with
his eyes closed and I was picking up Cramer's cigar. He
asked me if there was a program for him, and I said no.

"Sit down," I told him. "There soon will be. As you
know, Mr. Wolfe thinks better with his eyes shut."

The eyes opened. "I'm not thinking. There's nothing to
think about. There is no program."

That's what I was afraid of. "That's too bad," I said
sympathetically. "Of course if Johnny was still around it
would be worse because you would have five of us to think
up errands for instead of only four."

He snorted. "That's bootless, Archie. I'm quite aware
that Johnny was in my service when he died, and his dis-

regard of instructions didn't lift my onus. By no means. But Mr. Cramer and his army are at it now, and you would be lost in the stampede. The conviction of Peter Hays is going to be undone, and he knows it. He picked up the evidence that doomed him; now let him pick up the evidence that clears him."-

"If he does. What if he doesn't?"

"Then we'll see. Don't badger me. Go up and let Mrs. Molloy thank you properly for your intrepidity in saving her from annoyance. First rumple your hair as evidence of the fracas." Suddenly he roared, "Do you think I enjoy sitting here while that bull smashes through to the wretch I have goaded into two murders?"

I said distinctly, "I think you enjoy sitting here."

Saul asked sociably, "How about some pinochle, Archie?"

17

We didn't play pinochle for three nights and two days, but we might as well have. Friday night, Saturday, Saturday night, Sunday, and Sunday night.

It was not a vacuum. Things happened. Albert Freyer spent an hour with Wolfe Saturday morning, got a full report on the situation, and walked out on air. He even approved of letting the cops take it from there, since it was a cinch they couldn't nail the killer of Johnny Keems and Ella Reyes without unnailing Peter Hays. James R. Herold phoned twice a day, and Sunday afternoon came in person and brought his wife along. She taught me once more that you should never seal your verdict until the facts are in. I was sure she would be a little rooster-pecked specimen, and she was little, but in the first three minutes it became clear that at pecking time she went on the theory that it was more blessed to give than to receive. I won't say that I reversed the field on him entirely, but I understood him better. If and when he mentioned again that his wife was getting impatient I would know where my sympathy belonged if I had any to spare. Also he brought her after four o'clock, when he knew Wolfe would be up in the plant rooms, which was both intelligent and prudent. I made out fairly well with her, and when they left we still had a client.

Patrick A. Degan phoned Saturday morning and came for a talk at six o'clock. Apparently his main concern was to find out from Selma Molloy what her attitude was toward the $327,640.00, and he tried to persuade her that she would be a sap to pass it up, but he took the opportunity to discuss other developments with Wolfe and me. It had got in the paper, the *Gazette*, that Nero Wolfe's assistant, Archie Goodwin, had been at the morgue to look at the body of Ella Reyes, and that therefore there was probably some connection between her and Johnny Keems, though the police refused to say so, and Degan wanted to know. The interview ended on a sour note when Wolfe commented that it was natural for Degan to show an interest in that detail, since Ella Reyes had been Mrs. Irwin's maid and Degan was on familiar terms with Mrs. Irwin. When that warmed Degan up under the collar, Wolfe tried to explain that the word "familiar" implied undue intimacy only when it was intended to, and that he had given no reason for inferring such an intention, but Degan hadn't cooled off much when he left.

Since we wanted to keep informed fully and promptly on the progress of Cramer and his army, and therefore had to be on speaking terms, we graciously permitted Sergeant Stebbins an audience with Mrs. Molloy Saturday afternoon, and he was with her three hours, and Fritz served refreshments. We were pleased to hear later, from her, that Purley had spent a good third of the time on various aspects of the death of her husband, such as possible motives for Arkoff or Irwin to want him removed. The Molloy case had definitely been taken off the shelf. From the questions Purley asked it was evident that no one had been eliminated and no one had been treed. When I asked him, as he departed, if they were getting warm, he was so impolite that I knew the temperature had gone down rather than up.

Saturday evening Selma ate with us in the di[...] and Sunday at one she joined us again for chicken fri[...] with dumplings, Methodist style. Fritz is not a Methodist, but his dumplings are plenty good enough for angels.

Saul Panzer and Orrie Cather spent the two days visiting with former friends of Molloy's, spreading out from the list Patrick Degan had supplied, and concentrating on digging up a hint of the source of the third of a million in the safe-deposit box. Saul thought he might have found one Sunday morning, but it petered out. Fred Durkin plugged away at William Lesser and got enough material to fill three magazines, but none of it showed a remote connection with either the Arkoffs or Irwins, and that was essential. However, Fred got results, of a kind. Sunday afternoon, while I was down in the basement with Selma, teaching her how to handle a billiard cue, the doorbell rang, and I went up to find Fritz conversing through the crack permitted by the chain bolt, with Delia's Bill. It was my first contact with a suspect for many hours, and I felt like greeting him with a cordial handshake, but he wasn't having any. He was twice as grim as he had been before. In the office he stood with his fists on his hips and read the riot act. He had found out who the guy was going around asking about him, and that he worked for Nero Wolfe, and so did I, and the guff about the magazine article had been a blind, and he damn well wanted to know. It was rather confused the way he put it, and not clear at all exactly what he wanted to know, but I got the general idea. He was sore.

Neither of us got any satisfaction out of it. For him, I wouldn't apologize or promise to lock Wolfe and myself up for kidding Delia Brandt and damaging his reputation; and for me, he wasn't answering questions. He wasn't even hearing questions. He wouldn't even tell me when they were going to be married. I finally eased him to the hall and along to the door and on out, and went back to the basement to resume the billiard lesson.

Late that evening, Sunday, Inspector Cramer turned up, and when, after he got his big broad behind deposited in the red leather chair, Wolfe invited him to have some beer and he accepted, I knew he didn't have to be asked

... ing out. They weren't. He takes ... en he wants it understood that he's ... ould be treated accordingly. He tried to ... se he had no club to use, but what it ... as that he had got nowhere at all after two ... o days, and he wanted the fact or facts that Wolfe ... eserving for future use.

Wolfe didn't have any, and said so. But that didn't satisfy Cramer, and never will, on account of certain past occasions, so it ended with him bouncing up, his glass still half full of beer, and tramping out.

When I returned from closing the door after him I told Wolfe cheerfully, "Forget it, he's just tired. In the morning he'll be back on the job, full of whatever he's full of. In a month or so he'll pick up a trail, and by August he'll have it wrapped up. Of course by that time Peter Hays will be electrocuted, but what the hell, they can apologize to his father and mother and two sis—"

"Shut up, Archie."

"Yes, sir. If I wasn't afraid to leave Mrs. Molloy alone here with you I'd resign. This job is too dull. In fact, it doesn't seem to be a job."

"It will be." He took in air down to his waist, or where it would have been if he had one. When it was out he muttered, "It will have to be. When you become insufferable something has to be done. Have Saul and Fred and Orrie here at eight in the morning."

I locked the safe, made my desk neat, and went up to my room to call the boys from there, leaving him sitting behind his desk, an ideal model for an oversized martyr.

In a way he has spoiled me. Some of the spectacular charades he has thought up have led me to expect too much, and it was something of a letdown Monday morning when I learned what the program was. Nothing but another treasure hunt, and not even a safe-deposit box. I admit that it did the trick, but at the time it struck me as a damned small mouse to come out of so big a mountain.

I had made sacrifices, having rolled out early enough to finish my breakfast by the time Saul and Fred and Orrie arrived at eight, only to find that it hadn't been necessary when Wolfe told me on the house phone to bring them up at a quarter to nine. When the time came I led the way up the two flights and found his door standing open, and we entered. He was seated at the table near a window, his breakfast gone, but still with coffee, with the morning *Times* propped on the reading rack. He greeted the staff and asked me if there was any news, and I said no, I had phoned Stebbins and he had not bitten my ear off only because you can't bite over the wire.

He took a sip of coffee and put the cup down. "Then we'll have to try. You will go, all four, to Mrs. Molloy's apartment, and search it, covering every inch. Take probes for the upholstery and whatever tools may be required. The devil of it is you won't know what you're looking for."

"Then how will we know when we find it?"

"You won't, with any certainty. But we know that a situation existed which led to Molloy's murder; that he had cached a large sum of money in a safe-deposit box under an alias; that he was contemplating departure from the country; and that exhaustive inquiry among his friends and associates has disclosed no hint of where the money came from or when or how he got it. Further, there was no such hint found on his person, or among the papers taken from his office, or in his apartment, or in the safe-deposit box. I don't believe it. I do not believe that no such hint exists. As I said to Archie on Friday, when a man is involved in a circumstance pressing enough to cause his murder he must leave a relic of it somewhere, and I had hoped it was in that box. When it wasn't I should have persisted, but other matters intervened—for one thing, a woman got killed."

He took a sip of coffee. "We want that relic. It could be a portfolio, a notebook, a single slip of paper. It could be some object other than a record on paper, though I have no idea what. There are of course numberless places he could have left it—with some friend, checked at a hotel or other public place—but first we'll try his apartment, since it is as likely as any and is accessible. Regarding each article you see and touch you must ask yourselves, 'Could this possibly be it?' Archie, you will explain the matter to Mrs. Molloy, ask if she wishes to accompany you, and if not get her permission and the key. That's all, gentlemen. I don't ask if you have any questions, since I wouldn't know the answers to them. Archie, leave the phone number on my desk, in case I need to get you."

We went. I turned off one flight down. I knew she was up, since Fritz had delivered her breakfast tray. By then I was on sufficiently familiar terms with her—the word "familiar" implying no undue intimacy—to have a private knock, 2-1-2, and I used it and was told to enter. She was in a dressing gown or house gown or negligee or dishabille—anyway, it was soft and long and loose and lemon-colored—and without make-up. Without lipstick her mouth was even better than with. A habit of observation of minor details is an absolute must for a detective. We exchanged good mornings and I told her there had been no developments worth mentioning, but there was a program. When I explained it she said she didn't believe there could be anything in the apartment she didn't know about, but I reminded her that she hadn't even bothered to open the cartons that had come from the office, and asked if she had got rid of Molloy's clothing and other effects. She said no, she hadn't felt like touching them, and nothing had been taken away. I told her the search would be extremely thorough, and she said she didn't mind. I asked if she wanted to go along, and she said no.

"You'll think I'm crazy," she said, "after my not wanting to come here, but now I never want to enter that door again. I guess that was one thing that was wrong with me—I should have got out of there."

I told her that the only thing that had been wrong with her was that she thought Peter Hays had killed Molloy, whereas now she didn't, got the keys from her, went downstairs, where the hired help was waiting for me in the hall, put the phone number on Wolfe's desk, told Fritz where we were going, and left. Saul and Fred had assembled a kit of tools from the cupboard in the office where we kept an assortment of everything from keys to jimmies.

If I described every detail of our performance in the

Molloy apartment that day between 9:35 A.M. and 3:10
P.M. you might get some useful pointers on how to look
for a lost diamond or postage stamp, but if you haven't
lost a diamond or a postage stamp it wouldn't interest
you. When we got through we knew a lot of things: that
Molloy had hoarded old razor blades in a cardboard box
in his dresser; that someone had once upon a time burned
a little hole in the under side of a chair cushion, probably
with a cigarette, and at a later time someone had stuffed
a piece of lemon peel in the hole, God knew why; that
there were three loose tiles in the bathroom wall and a
loose board in the living-room floor; that Mrs. Molloy had
three girdles, liked pale yellow underwear and white night-
ies, used four different shades of nylons, and kept no letters except those from a sister who lived in Arkansas; that
apparently there were no unpaid bills other than one for
$3.84 from a laundry; that none of the pieces of furniture
had hollow legs; that if a jar of granulated sugar slips from
your hand and spills you have a problem; and a thousand
others. Saul and I together went over every scrap of the
contents of the three cartons, already inspected by Orrie.

It would be misleading to say we found nothing whatever. We found two empty drawers. They were the two
top drawers, one on each side, of a desk against the wall
of what Molloy might have called his den. None of the
six keys Selma had given me fitted their locks, which were
good ones, Wetherbys, and Saul had to work on them
with the assortment in the kit. The drawers were as
empty as the day they were built, and had presumably
been locked from force of habit.

At 3:10 P.M. I used the phone there in the apartment
and told Wolfe the bad news, including the empty drawers.
Orrie said to tell him that never had so many searched
so long for so little, but it didn't appeal to me. Wolfe
told me to tell Fred and Orrie that was all for the day
and to bring Saul in with me. After making a tour to
verify that we were leaving things as we had found them,
we moved out. Down on the sidewalk we parted, Fred and
Orrie heading for the corner to get a drink to drown the
disappointment, and Saul and I, with the kit of tools,
flagging a taxi. It wasn't a cheerful ride. If the best the

genius could do was start us combing the metropolitan area, including Jersey and Long Island, for a relic that might not exist, the future wasn't very bright.

But he had something a little more specific. We had barely crossed the sill to the office when he blurted at me, "About that Delia Brandt. About Molloy's proposal to her of a trip to South America. You said last Wednesday that she told you she had put him off, but you thought she lied. Why did you think she lied?"

I stood. "The way she said it, the way she looked, the way she answered questions about it. And just her. I had formed an opinion of her."

"Have you changed your opinion? Since she is going to marry William Lesser?"

"Hell no. She couldn't go to South America with a dead man, and evidently, from Fred's reports, she was playing Lesser all the time on an option. If Lesser found out what the score was and decided to take—"

"That's not my target. If Molloy was preparing to decamp and take that girl with him, and if she had agreed to go, he might have entrusted certain objects to her care—for example, some of the objects he removed from the empty drawers you found. Is it fantastic to assume that he left them in her apartment for safekeeping pending departure?"

"No, not fantastic. I wouldn't trust her with a subway token, but apparently his opinion of her wasn't the same flavor as mine. It's quite possible."

"Then you and Saul will go and search her apartment. Now."

When Wolfe gets desperate he is absolutely fearless. He will expose me to the risk of a five-year stretch up the river without batting an eye. That's okay, since I am old enough to vote and can always say no, but that time he was inviting another party too, so I turned to look at Saul. He merely asked, "Will she be there?"

"If she's working, probably not until around five-thirty, maybe later. If she's there I might be able to take her out to buy champagne, but then you'd have to do the work. Shall I phone?"

"You might as well."

I went to my desk and dialed the number, waited through fifteen whirrs, hung up, and swiveled. "No answer. If you like the idea, we won't want the kit, just some of the keys. The door downstairs has a Manson lock, old style. The one to her apartment is a Wyatt. You know more about them than I do."

Saul brought the kit to my desk and opened it, selected four strings of keys and dropped them in his pocket, and closed the kit. While he was doing that I went to the cupboard and got two pairs of rubber gloves.

"I must remind you," Wolfe said as we started out, "that prudence is no shame to valor. I shall not evade my responsibility as accessory."

"Much obliged," I thanked him. "If we're caught we'll say you begged us not to."

We went to Ninth Avenue for a taxi, and on the way downtown discussed modus operandi. Not that it needed much discussion. Dismissing the cab on Christopher Street, we walked on to Arbor Street, rounded the corner, and continued to Number 43. Nobody had painted it in the five days since I had seen it. We entered the vestibule, and I pushed the button marked Brandt. Getting no click, I pushed it again, and, after another wait, a third time.

"Okay," I told Saul, and stepped to the outer door, which was standing open, for an outlook. Arbor Street is not Fifth Avenue, and only two boys and a woman with a dog had passed by when Saul told my back, "Come on in." It had taken him about a minute and a half. We entered.

He preceded me up the narrow dingy stairs, the idea being that we would do a quick once-over and then I would stand guard outside, at the head of the stairs, while he dug deeper. As we reached the top of the third flight he had a string of keys in his hand, ready to tackle the Wyatt, but I remembered that prudence is no shame to valor and went to the door first and knocked. I waited, knocked louder, got no response, and stepped aside for Saul. The Wyatt took longer than the one downstairs, perhaps three minutes. When he got it he pushed the door open. Since I was supposed to be in command, the proper thing would have been for him to let me go in first, but he crossed the threshold, saying, "Jumping Jesus."

I was at his elbow, staring with him. At my former visit it had been one of those rooms that call for expert dodging to get anywhere. Now it would have taken more than dodging. The piano bench was still where it belonged, in the center of the main traffic lane, and the other pieces of furniture were more or less in place, but otherwise it was a first-rate mess. Cushions had been ripped open and the stuffing pulled out and scattered around; books and magazines were off their shelves and helter-skelter on the floor; flowerpots had been dumped and dropped; and the general effect was about what you would get if you turned a room over to a dozen orangoutangs and told them to enjoy themselves.

"He didn't leave it as neat as we—"I started to comment, and stopped. Saul had spotted it too, and we moved together, on past the piano bench. It was Delia Brandt, on the floor near the couch where I had sat with her. She was on her face, her legs stretched out. I squatted on one side and Saul on the other, but one feel of her bare forearm was enough to show that no tests were necessary. She had been dead at least twelve hours and probably longer. We didn't look for a wound because that wasn't necessary either. A cord as thick as a clothesline was tight around her neck.

We got erect and I stepped through the clutter to a doorway, the door standing open, for a look at the bedroom, while Saul went and closed the door to the hall. The bedroom was even worse, with the bed torn apart, the innards of the mattress all over, and clothing and other objects sprayed around. A glance in the bathroom showed that it had not been neglected. Back in the living room, Saul was standing looking down at her.

"He killed her," he said, "before he started looking. Stuff from cushions on top of her."

"Yeah, so I noticed. He worked the bedroom and closets too, so there's nothing left for us except one thing. She's got her clothes on. Either he found it or something scared him out or what he was after was too bulky to be on her."

"The clothes women wear nowadays he wouldn't have

to take them off. Why the gloves? Going to rake through
the leavings?"

"No. Put them on." I handed him a pair, and started
pulling mine on. "We'll try the one thing he left. Unless
you've got a date."

"You don't make prints on clothes."

"You don't make prints on anything with gloves on."
I got my knife from my pocket, opened it, squatted,
slipped two fingers under the neck of the blouse, and slit
it down to the waist. Saul, squatting on the other side,
unzipped the skirt and moved to the feet to take the
hem and pull the skirt off. I told him to look at the shoes,
which were house sandals, tied on, and he did so, removing
them and tossing them aside. The slip was as simple as
the blouse. I cut the straps and slit it down the back from
top to bottom and pushed it to either side. The pants
were simple too; I got my fingers inside under the hips,
and Saul worked them down and off. The girdle was
slower, since I didn't care to scratch the skin. Saul squatted
on the other side again and helped me keep it lifted
enough to slit it and leave her intact.

"She's good and cold," he said.

"Yeah. Stuff the edges under and we'll roll her over to
you."

He did so, and with one hand under a hip and the other
under a shoulder I rolled her, and Saul eased her as she
came, and she was on her back. That way, face up, it was
something else. The face of a girl who was strangled to
death twelve or fourteen hours ago is not a girl's face.
Saul covered it with what was left of a cushion and then
helped me finish the operation. There was nothing between the blouse and the slip, and nothing between the
slip and the girdle, and nothing between the girdle and
the skin, but when I lifted the brassiere and she was
naked, there it was, fastened between the breasts with
tape. A key. I pulled it loose, pulled the tape off, gave it
a look, said, "Grand Central locker, out quick," went to
the bedroom for a blanket, and came back and covered
her. Saul was at the door, peeling his gloves off, and I had
mine off by the time I joined him. He used one of his
to turn the doorknob, and, in the hall, to pull the door

shut. The spring lock clicked and we made for the stairs.

We saw no one on the way down, but as we stepped out
to the sidewalk a man turned in, evidently a tenant, as he
gave us a glance. However, he was two seconds too late
to be able to swear that we had been inside the house.
When we had turned the corner and were on Christopher
Street, Saul asked, "Walking for our health?"

"I could use some health after that," I told him. "I
suppose it doesn't matter how you do it if you do it, but
some ways seem worse than others. At Seventh Avenue
we'll split. One of us will take the subway and shuttle to
Grand Central, and the other will phone Centre Street
and go and report to Wolfe. Which do you prefer?"

"I'll take Grand Central."

"Okay." I handed him the locker key. "But it's possible
there's an eye on it, no telling whose. You'd better give
me the keys and gloves."

He transferred them to my pocket as we walked. At
Seventh Avenue he went for the subway stairs and I
entered the cigar store at the corner, found the phone
booth, dialed SP 7-3100, and, when I got a voice, whined
into the transmitter, high and thin, "Name and address,
Delia Brandt, B-R-A-N-D-T, Forty-three Arbor Street, Manhattan. Got it?"

"Yes. What—"

"I'm telling you. I think she's dead. In her apartment.
You'd better hurry." I hung up, heard the rattle, felt in
the coin-return cup to see if the machine had swallowed
the wrong way because you never know, departed, and
got a taxi.

When I got out in front of the old brownstone it was
a quarter to five, precisely one hour since Wolfe had told
us he wouldn't evade his responsibility as accessory. With
the chain bolt on as usual during my absence, Fritz had
to come to let me in, and after one glance at my face he
said, "Ah."

"Right," I told him. "Ah it is. But I don't want you to
be an accessory too, so if they ask you how I looked say
just like always, debonair."

In the office I put the gloves and strings of keys away
and then went to my desk and buzzed the plant rooms.

He must have been hard at work, for it took him a while to answer.

"Yes?"

"Sorry to disturb you, but I thought you ought to know that it's more serious than breaking and entering. It's also disturbing a body in a death by violence. Her apartment looked as if a hurricane had hit it, and she was on the floor, dead and cold. Strangled. We took her clothes off and found a key to a Grand Central checking locker taped to her skin, and took it and left. I phoned the police from a booth, and Saul has gone to Grand Central to see what's in the locker. He should be here in about twenty minutes."

"When did she die?"

"More than twelve hours ago. That's the best I can do."

"What time was William Lesser here yesterday?"

"Four-forty."

Silence. Then: "There is nothing to say or do until we learn what is in the locker. If it is merely another fortune in currency—But speculation is idle. Whatever it is, you and Saul will examine it."

I choked the temptation to ask if he wanted us to bring it up to the plant rooms. He would have had to say no, and to pile that on top of the news of another corpse would have been hitting him when he was down. But I had no ironclad rules between me and normal conduct, so when he hung up I went out to the stoop to wait for Saul. I even went down the seven steps to the sidewalk. Two neighborhood kids who were playing catch on the pavement stopped, stepped onto the opposite curb, and stood watching me. That house and its occupants had been centers of attraction, either sinister or merely mysterious, I wasn't sure which, ever since a boy named Pete Drossos had been let in by me for a conference with Wolfe and had got murdered the next day. By the time I looked at my wristwatch the tenth time the situation was a little strained, with them standing there staring at me, and I was about ready to retreat to an inside post behind the glass panel when a taxi came rolling up and stopped at the curb, and Saul climbed out, after paying the driver, with a medium-sized black leather suitcase dangling in his hand. Letting him have the honor of delivering the bacon, I followed him up the steps and on in. He took it to the office and put it on a chair.

At a glance it had been manhandled. The lock had been pried open, not by an expert, and it was held shut only by the catches at the ends. I asked Saul, "Do you want to tell me or shall I tell you?"

"You tell me."

"Glad to. Wolfe guessed right. Molloy had it stowed in her apartment, and after his death, maybe right away or maybe only yesterday, she busted it open and took a look." I hefted it. "Another deduction: she didn't clean it out. Because if she had why should she stash it in a locker and tape the key to her hide, and also because it's not empty. Wolfe says we're to examine it, but first, I think, for prints."

I went to the cupboard and got things and we set to work. We weren't as expert as the scientist had been with the safe-deposit box, but when we got through we had an assortment of photographs marked with locations that were nothing to be ashamed of. Of course they were only for future reference, since we had no samples of anybody for comparison. After putting them in envelopes and putting things away, we placed the suitcase on my desk and opened it.

It was about two-thirds full of a mixed collection. There were shirts and ties, probably his favorites that he couldn't bear to leave, a pair of slippers, six tubes of Cremasine for shaving, two suits of pajamas, socks and handkerchiefs, and other miscellaneous personal items. Stacking them on the desk, we came to a bulging leather briefcase. It should have been dusted for prints too, but we were too warm to wait, and I lifted it out, opened it, and extracted the contents.

It wasn't a relic, it was a whole museum. Saul pulled a chair up beside mine, and we went through it together. I won't describe the items, or even list them, because it would take too long and also because it was Wolfe who had guessed where they were and he should have the pleasure of showing them. We had just reached the bottom of the pile when six o'clock brought Wolfe down from the plant rooms. He started for his desk, veered to come to mine, and glared down at the haberdashery.

"That's just packing," I told him. I tapped the pile of papers. "Here it is. Enough relics to choke a camel."

He picked it up and circled around his desk to his chair and started in. Saul and I put the rest of the stuff back in the suitcase and closed it, and then sat and watched. For ten minutes the only sounds were rustlings of the papers and Wolfe's occasional grunts. He had nearly reached the bottom of the stack when the phone rang and I answered it.

"Nero Wolfe's office, Archie Good—"

"This is Stebbins. About a woman named Brandt, Delia Brandt. When did you see her last?"

"Hold it a second while I sneeze." I covered the transmitter and turned. "Stebbins asking about Delia Brandt, if you're interested." Wolfe frowned, hesitated, took his phone, and put it to his ear. I uncovered the transmitter and sneezed at it and then spoke.

"I hope I'm not going to have a cold. The last one I had—"

"Quit stalling," he snarled. "I asked you a question."

"I know you did, and you ought to know better by this time. If there's any good reason, or even a poor one, why I should answer questions about a woman named Delia Brandt, what is it?"

"Her body has been found in her apartment. Murdered. Your name and address are on the memo page in her phone book, the last entry. When did you see her last?"

"My God. She's dead?"

"Yeah. When you're murdered you're dead. Quit stalling."

"I'm not stalling. If I didn't react you might think I killed her myself. The first and last time I saw her was last Wednesday evening around nine-thirty, at her apartment. We were collecting background on Molloy, and she was his secretary for ten months, up to the time he died. I had a brief talk with her on the phone late Thursday afternoon. That's all."

"You were just collecting background?"

"Right."

"We'd like to have you come and tell us what you collected. Now."

"Where are you?"

"At Homicide West. I just got here with a man named William Lesser. When did you see him last?"

"Give me a reason. I always need a reason."

"Yeah, I know. He came to Delia Brandt's apartment twenty minutes ago and found us there. He says he had a date with her. He also says he thinks you killed her. Is that a good enough reason? When did you see him last?"

I never got to answer that. Wolfe's voice broke in.

"Mr. Stebbins, this is Nero Wolfe. I would like to speak with Mr. Cramer."

"He's busy." I swear Purley got hoarser the instant he heard Wolfe. "We want Goodwin down here."

"Not until I have spoken with Mr. Cramer."

Silence; then: "Hold it. I'll see."

We waited. I looked at Wolfe, but it was one-way because his eyes were closed. He opened them only when Cramer's voice came.

"You there, Wolfe? Cramer. What do you want?"

"I want to expose a murderer, and I'm ready to. If you wish to be present, bring Mr. and—"

"I'm coming there right now!"

"No. I have to study some documents. You wouldn't get in. Come at nine o'clock, and bring Mr. and Mrs. Irwin and Mr. and Mrs. Arkoff—and you may as well bring Mr. Lesser. He deserves to be in the audience. The others must be. Nine o'clock."

"Goddam it, I want to know—"

"You will, but not now. I have work to do."

He cradled his phone, and I followed suit. He spoke. "Archie, phone Mr. Freyer, Mr. Degan, and Mr. Herold. If he wishes to bring his wife he may. For this sort of thing the bigger the audience the better. And inform Mrs. Molloy."

"Mrs. Molloy won't be here."

"She is here."

"I mean she won't be in the audience, not if Herold is. She doesn't know Peter Hays is Paul Herold, and let him tell her if and when he wants to. Anyway she doesn't want to be with people, and you don't need her."

"Very well." He leered at me. He may have thought it was a tender glance of sympathy, but I call it a leer. "It is understood, of course, that you were not there today. If an explanation of how I got this material is required I'll supply it."

"Then that's all for me?" Saul asked.

"No. You'll be at his elbow. He has degenerated into a maniac. If you'll dine with us? Now I must digest this stuff."

He went back to the pile of papers.

13

The host was late to the party, but it wasn't his fault. I wasn't present at the private argument Cramer insisted on having with Wolfe in the dining room, being busy elsewhere, but as I passed in the hall, admitting guests as they arrived, I could hear their voices through the closed door. Since the door to the office was soundproofed and I kept it shut, they weren't audible in there.

The red leather chair was of course reserved for Inspector Cramer, and Purley Stebbins was on one nearby against the wall, facing the gathering. Jerome and Rita Arkoff and Tom and Fanny Irwin were in the front row, where Saul and I had spaced the chairs, but Irwin had moved his close to his wife's—not, however, taking her hand to hold. Mr. and Mrs. Herold and Albert Freyer were grouped over by the globe, off apart. Back of the Arkoffs and Irwins were William Lesser and Patrick Degan, and between them and slightly to the rear was Saul Panzer. That way the path from me to Degan was unobstructed and Saul was only an arm's length from him.

It was a quarter past nine, and the silence, broken only by a mutter here and there, was getting pretty heavy when the door opened and Wolfe and Cramer entered. Wolfe crossed to his desk and sat, but Cramer stood to make a speech.

"I want you to understand," he told them, "that this is not an official inquiry. Five of you came here at my request, but that's all it was, a request. Sergeant Stebbins and I are here as observers, and we take no responsibility for anything Nero Wolfe says or does. As it stands now, you can walk out whenever you feel like it."

"This is a little irregular, isn't it, Inspector?" Arkoff asked.

"I said you can walk out," Cramer told him. He stood a moment, turned and sat, and scowled at Wolfe.

Wolfe was taking them in. "I'm going to begin," he said conversationally, "by reporting a coincidence, though it is unessential. It is unessential, but not irrelevant. Reading the *Times* at breakfast this morning, I noticed a Washington dispatch on page one." He picked up a newspaper from his desk. "If you'll indulge me I'll read some of it:

> "A total disclosure law requiring all private welfare and pension plans to open books to governmental inspection was recommended today by a Senate subcommittee. The proposal was based on a two-year study that disclosed practices ranging from sloppy bookkeeping to a $900,000 embezzlement.
>
> "The funds have grown to the point, the committee said, that they now provide benefits to 29,000,000 workers and to 46,000,000 dependents of these workers. Assets of the pension funds alone now total about 25 billion dollars, it was said.
>
> "The Senate group, headed by Senator Paul H. Douglas, Democrat of Illinois, said: 'While the great majority of welfare and pension programs are being responsibly and honestly administered, the rights and equities of the beneficiaries in many instances are being dangerously ignored. In other cases, the funds of the programs are being dissipated and at times become the hunting ground of the unscrupulous.' "

Wolfe put the paper down. "It goes on, but that will do. I read it for the record and because it juxtaposed two things: the word 'welfare' and large sums of money. For a solid week I had been trying to find a hint to start me on the trail of the man who killed Michael Molloy—and subsequently Johnny Keems and Ella Reyes—enough of one at least to stir my pulse, to no avail. This, if not a flare, was at least a spark. Patrick Degan was the head of an organization called the Mechanics Alliance Welfare Association, and a large sum of money had been found in a safe-deposit box Molloy had rented under an assumed name."

He pushed the newspaper aside. "That faint hint, patiently and persistently pursued, might eventually have led me to the truth, but luckily it wasn't needed. I have here in my drawer a sheaf of papers which contain evidence of these facts: that from nineteen-fifty-one to nineteen-fifty-five Molloy made purchases of small pieces of land in various parts of the country; that their value, and the amounts of money he had to put up, were negligible; that in each case the purchaser of record was some 'camp'—examples are the Wide World Children's Camp and the Blue Sky Children's Camp; that these camps, twenty eight in all, borrowed a total of nearly two million dollars from Mr. Degan's organization on mortgages; that Molloy's share of the loot was one-fourth and Degan's share three-fourths, from which each had presumably to meet certain expenses; and that the date of the last such loan on mortgage was October seventeenth, nineteen-fifty-five. I can supply many details, but those are the essentials. Do you wish to comment, Mr. Degan?"

Of course all eyes were on him, but his were only for Wolfe. "No," he said, "except that it's outrageous and libelous and I'll get your hide. Produce your sheaf of papers."

Wolfe shook his head. "The District Attorney will produce them when the time comes. But I'll humor your curiosity. When Molloy decided to leave the country with his loot, alarmed by the Senate investigation, and to take his secretary, Delia Brandt, with him, he stowed his records in a suitcase and left it in Delia Brandt's apartment. That is suggestive, since prudence would have dic-

tated their destruction. It suggests that he foresaw some
future function for them, and the most likely one would
have been to escape penalty for himself by supplying
evidence against you. No doubt you foresaw that too, and
that's why you killed him. Do you wish to comment?"

"No. Go ahead and hang yourself."

"Wait a minute," Cramer snapped. "I want to see those
papers."

"Not now. By agreement I have an hour without interruption."

"Where did you get them?"

"Listen and you'll know." Wolfe returned to Degan.
"The best conjecture is that you knew Molloy had those
records, some in your writing, and you knew or suspected
he was preparing to decamp. If you demanded that he give
them to you or destroy them in your presence, he refused.
After you killed him you had no time to search the apartment, but enough to go through his clothing, and it must
have been a relief to find the key to the safe-deposit box,
since that was the most likely repository of the records—
but it was a qualified relief, since you didn't dare to use
the key. If you still have it, and almost certainly you have,
it can be found and will be a damaging bit of evidence.
You now have another, as the administrator of Molloy's
estate, but surely the safe-deposit company can distinguish
between the original and the duplicate they had to have
made—and by the way, what would you have done if,
opening the box in the presence of Mr. Goodwin and Mr.
Parker, you had found the records in it? Had you decided
on a course?"

Degan didn't reply. "Get on," Cramer rasped. "Where
did you get them?"

Wolfe ignored him. "However, they weren't there.
Another question: how did you dare to kill him when you
didn't know where they were? But I'll venture to answer
that myself. By getting Peter Hays there and giving the
police an obvious culprit, you insured plenty of time and
opportunity for searching the apartment as an old friend
of Mrs. Molloy's. She is not present to inform us, but that
can wait."

"Where is she?" Cramer demanded.

Ignored again. "You must admit, Mr. Degan, that luck was with you. For instance, the safe-deposit box. You had the key, but even if you had known the name Molloy had used in renting it, and you probably didn't, you wouldn't have dared to try to get at it. Then fortune intervened, represented by me. I got you access to the box. But in spite of that good fortune you weren't much better off, for the records weren't there, and until you found them you were in great jeopardy. What did you do? I wouldn't mind paying you the compliment of supposing that you conceived the notion that Molloy had cached the records in Delia Brandt's apartment, and you approached her, but I doubt if you deserve it. It is far more likely that she approached you; that, having decided to marry William Lesser, she wanted to get rid of Molloy's suitcase, still in her apartment; that before doing so she forced it open and inspected its contents; that if items such as passports and steamship or airplane tickets were there she destroyed them; that she examined the sheaf of papers and from them learned that there was a large sum of money somewhere and that you had been involved with Molloy in extensive and lucrative transactions and probably knew where the money was. She was not without cunning. Before approaching you she took the suitcase, with the records in it, to Grand Central Terminal and put it in a checking locker. Then she saw you, told you what she knew and what she had, and demanded the money."

"That's a lie!" William Lesser blurted.

Wolfe's eyes darted to him. "Then what did she do? Since you know?"

"I don't know, but I know she wouldn't do that! It's a lie!"

"Then let me finish it. A lie, like a truth, should reach its destination. And that, Mr. Degan, was where luck caught up with you. You couldn't give her the money from the safe-deposit box, but even if you gave her a part of your share of the loot and she surrendered the records to you, you couldn't empty her brain of what she knew, and as long as she lived she would be a threat. So last night you went to her apartment, ostensibly, I presume, to give her the money and get the records, but actually to kill her, and you did so. I don't know—*Saul!*"

I wouldn't say that Saul slipped up. Sitting between Lesser and Degan, naturally he was concentrating on Degan, and Lesser gave no warning. He just lunged, right across Saul's knees, either to grab Degan or hit him, or maybe both. By the time I got there Saul had his coattail, jerking him off, Degan was sitting on the floor, and Purley Stebbins was on the way. But Purley, who has his points, wasn't interested in Lesser, leaving him to Saul. He got his big paws on Degan's arm, helped him up, and helped him down again onto the chair, while Saul and I bulldozed Lesser to the couch. When we were placed again it was an improvement: Stebbins on one side of Degan and Saul on the other, and Lesser on the sidelines. Cramer, who had stood to watch the operation, sat down.

Wolfe resumed. "I was saying, Mr. Degan, that I don't know whether you searched her apartment for the records, but naturally—Did he, Mr. Cramer?"

"Someone did," Cramer growled. "Good. I'm stopping this right here. I want to see those records and I want to know how you got them."

Wolfe looked at the wall clock. "I still have thirty-eight minutes of my hour. If you interpose authority of course you have it. But I have your word. Is it garbage?"

Cramer's face got redder, and his jaw worked. "Go ahead."

"I should think so." Wolfe returned to Degan. "You did search, naturally, without success. You weren't looking for something as small as a key, but even if you had been you still wouldn't have found it, for it was destined for me. How it reached me is a detail Mr. Cramer may discuss with me later if he still thinks it worth while; all that concerns you is that I received it, and sent Mr. Panzer with it to Grand Central, and he returned with the suitcase. From it I got the sheaf of papers now in my drawer. I was inspecting them when Mr. Cramer phoned me shortly after six o'clock, and I arranged with him for this meeting. That's all, Mr. Degan."

Wolfe's eyes went left, and his voice lifted and sharpened. "Now for you, Mrs. Irwin. I wonder if you know how deep your hole is?"

"Don't say anything, Fanny." Irwin stood up. "We're going. Come on, Fanny." He took her shoulder and she came up to her feet.

"I think not," Wolfe said. "I quote Mr. Cramer: 'As it stands now, you can walk out whenever you feel like it.' But the standing has been altered. Archie, to the door. Mr. Cramer, I'll use restraint if necessary."

Cramer didn't hesitate. He was gruff. "I think you'd better stay and hear it out, Mr. Irwin."

"I refuse to, Inspector. I'm not going to sit here while he insults and bullies my wife."

"Then you can stand. Stay at the door, Goodwin. No one leaves this room until I say so. That's official. All right, Wolfe. God help you if you haven't got it."

Wolfe looked at her. "You might as well sit down, Mrs. Irwin. That's better. You already know most of what I'm going to tell you, perhaps all. Last Wednesday evening a man named Keems, in my employ, called at your apartment and spoke with you and your husband. You were leaving for a party and cut the interview short. Keems left the building with you, but soon he went back to your apartment and talked with your maid, Ella Reyes, and gave her a hundred dollars in cash. In return she gave him information. She told him that on January third you complained of no headache until late in the afternoon, immediately after you received a phone call from Patrick Degan. She may even—"

"That isn't true." Fanny Irwin had to squeeze it out.

"If you mean she didn't tell him that, I admit I can't prove it, since Johnny Keems and Ella Reyes are both dead. If you mean that didn't happen, I don't believe you. She may even have also told him that she heard the phone conversation on an extension, and that Mr. Degan told you to withdraw from the theater party that evening, giving a headache as an excuse, and to suggest that Mrs. Molloy be invited in your stead."

"You know what you're saying," Jerome Arkoff said darkly.

"I do," Wolfe told Mrs. Irwin, not him. "I am charging

you with complicity in the murder of Michael Molloy, and, by extension, of Johnny Keems and Ella Reyes and Delia Brandt. With that information from your maid, Keems, ignoring the instructions I had given him, sought out Degan. Degan, seeing that he was in great and imminent peril, acted promptly and effectively. On some pretext, probably of taking Keems to interview some other person, he had Keems wait for him at a place not frequented at that time of night while he went for his car; and instead of going for his car he stole one, drove it to the appointed place, and killed Keems with it."

Wolfe's head moved. "Do you wish to challenge that detail, Mr. Degan? Have you an alibi for that night?"

"I'm listening," Degan said, louder than necessary. "And don't forget others are listening too."

"I won't." Wolfe returned to Fanny Irwin. "But Degan had learned from Keems the source of his information, and Ella Reyes was almost as great a menace as Keems had been. Whether he communicated with her directly or through you, I don't know. He arranged to meet her, and killed her, and put the body where it was not found until somewhat later, taking her handbag to delay identification. By then he was no better than a maniac, and when, two or three days afterward, he was confronted with still another threat, this time from Delia Brandt, qualms, either of conscience or of trepidation, bothered him not at all. But I wonder about you. You felt no qualms? You feel none?"

"Don't say anything," her husband told her. He had her hand.

"I'm not sure that's good advice," Wolfe said. "There are certainly people present who would question it. If you'll turn your head, madam, to your right and rear, there by the big globe—the man on the left and the woman beside him—they are the parents of Peter Hays, who has been convicted of a murder you helped to commit. The other man is also deeply interested; he is Peter Hays's counsel. Now if you'll turn your head the other way. The man on the couch, who lost control of himself a few minutes ago, is—or was—the fiancé of Delia Brandt. They were to be married—tomorrow, Mr. Lesser?"

No reply.

Wolfe didn't press him. "And standing at the door is Archie Goodwin, and on Mr. Degan's left is Saul Panzer. They were friends and colleagues of Johnny Keems—and I myself knew Keems for some years and had esteem for him. I'm sorry I can't present to you any of the friends or family of Ella Reyes; you knew her better than anyone else here."

"What the hell good does this do?" Jerome Arkoff demanded.

Wolfe ignored it. "The point is this, Mrs. Irwin. Mr. Degan is done for. I have this sheaf of papers in my drawer. The key for the safe-deposit box which he took from Molloy's body will almost certainly be found in Degan's possession. There are other items—for example, when Mr. Goodwin left this house last Tuesday a man followed him, and that man will be found and will tell who engaged him. I'll stake my reputation that it was Degan. Now that we know that Degan killed those four people, the evidence will pile up. Fingerprints in Delia Brandt's apartment, his movements Wednesday night and Thursday night and Sunday night, an examination of the books of his organization; it will be overwhelming."

"What do you want of me?" she asked. They were her first words since he had called her a murderer.

"I want you to consider your position. Your husband advises you to say nothing, but he should consider it too. You are clearly open to a charge as accessory to murder. If you think you must not admit that Degan phoned you on January third, and suggested that you withdraw from the theater party and that Mrs. Molloy be asked in your stead, you are wrong. Such an admission would injure you only if it carried the implication that you knew why Degan wanted Mrs. Molloy away from her apartment—knew it either when he made the suggestion or afterward. And such an implication is not inherent. It is even implausible, since Degan wouldn't want to disclose his intention to commit murder. He could have told you merely that he wanted a private conversation with you and asked you to make an opportunity for that evening, and his suggestion of Mrs. Molloy could have been offhand. If so, it is unwise and dangerous for you to keep silent, for silence can carry implications too. If Degan merely wanted an opportunity to discuss some private matter—"

"That was it!" she said, for all to hear.

Her husband let go of her hand.

Jerome Arkoff croaked, "Don't be a goddam fool, Tom! This is for keeps!"

Rita sang out, "Go on, Fanny! Spit it out!"

Fanny offered both hands to her husband, and he took them. She gave him her eyes too. "You know me, Tom. You know I'm yours. He just said he had to see me, he had to tell me something. He came to the apartment, but now I see, because he didn't come until nearly ten—"

Degan went for her. Of course it was a convulsion rather than a calculated movement. It couldn't very well have been calculated, since Saul and Purley were right there beside him, and since, even if he got his hands on her and somehow managed to finish her, it wouldn't have helped his prospects any. It was as Wolfe had said, after killing four people he was no better than a maniac, and, hearing her blurting out her contribution to his doom, he acted like one. He never touched her. Saul and Purley had him and jerked him back, and those two together are enough for any maniac.

Irwin was on his feet. So were the Arkoffs, and so was Cramer. Albert Freyer went loping over to my desk and reached for the phone.

Wolfe was speaking. "I'm through, Mr. Cramer. Twelve minutes short of my hour."

They didn't need me for a minute or two. I opened the door to the hall and went upstairs to report to Mrs. Molloy. She had it coming to her if anyone did. And from her room I could chase Freyer off the phone and call Lon Cohen at the Gazette and give him some news.

A few days later Cramer dropped in at six o'clock and called me Archie when I let him in. After getting settled in the red leather chair, accepting beer, and exchanging some news and views with Wolfe, he stated, not aggressively, "The District Attorney wants to know where and how you got the key to the locker. I wouldn't mind knowing myself."

"I think you would," Wolfe declared.

"Would what?"

"Would mind. It would only ruffle you to no purpose. If the District Attorney persists, and I tell him it came to me in the mail and the envelope has been destroyed, or that Archie found it on the sidewalk, what then? He has the murderer, and you delivered him. I doubt if you will persist."

He didn't.

The problem of the fee, which had to be settled as soon as Peter Hays had been turned loose, was a little more complicated. Having mentioned to James R. Herold, while under a strain, the sum of fifty thousand dollars, Wolfe wanted to stick to it, but fifty grand and expenses seemed pretty steep for a week's work, and besides, he was already in the 80% bracket. He solved it very neatly, arranging for Herold to donate a check for $16,666.67 to Johnny Keems's widow and one for the same amount to Ella Reyes' mother. That left $16,666.66, plus expenses, for Wolfe, and makes a monkey out of people who call him greedy, since he got only $16,666.66 instead of $16,666.67. And P.H., after he got from under, finally conceded that his father and mother were his parents, though the announcement of the wedding in the Times had it Peter Hays, and the Times is always right.

They were married a month or so after Patrick A. Degan had been convicted of first-degree murder, and a couple of weeks later they called at the office. I wouldn't have recognized P.H. as the guy I had seen that April day through the steel lattice. He looked comparatively human and even acted human. I want to be fair, but I also want to report accurately, and the fact is that he didn't impress me as any particular treat. When they got up to go Selma Hays moved to the corner of Wolfe's desk and said she had to kiss him. She said she doubted if he wanted to be kissed, but she simply had to.

Wolfe shook his head. "Let us forgo it. You wouldn't enjoy it and neither would I. Kiss Mr. Goodwin instead; that will be more to the point."

I was right there. She turned to me, and for a second she thought she was going to, and so did I. But as pink started to show in her cheeks she drew back, and I said something, I forget what. That girl has sense. Some risks are just too big to take.